…H AT A DROP-IN

…YRTLE CLOVER MYSTERY

ELIZABETH SPANN CRAIG

License Notes

This book is a work of fiction. With the exception of recognized historical figures, the characters in this novel are fictional. Any resemblance to actual persons, living or dead, is purely coincidental.

Formatting by RikHall.com
Cover Design by Scarlett Rugers
Editing by Judy Beatty

ISBN: 978-0-9895180-1-7

Acknowledgement

Thanks most of all to my family; especially Coleman, Riley, and Elizabeth Ruth; for their love and support.

Many thanks to my mother and father, Beth and Henry Spann, for beta reading Death at a Drop-In and to Judy Beatty for editing.
A special thanks to Scarlett Rugers for the cover design.
Thanks to Rik Hall for formatting the book for digital and print release.

And thanks as always to the writing community for its encouragement.

Dedication

To Mama and Daddy, with thanks and love.

DEATH AT A DROP-IN

Chapter One

"Miles?" asked Myrtle, peering closely at her friend. "Are you asking me on a date?"

"Certainly not!" said Miles, flustered. He pushed his rimless glasses higher on his nose.

"Then why are you asking me to go to a drop-in with you, if I'm not your date?" Myrtle was vastly relieved that Miles wasn't asking her out. She was in her eighties, widowed about forty years. She was pretty sure that she wouldn't be current on dating protocol.

"I simply don't want to go to this party by myself," said Miles with a sigh. He swirled the ice around in his tall glass of iced tea. They had just finished watching *Tomorrow's Promise*, a soap opera that Myrtle had somehow gotten him hooked on. Today's installment had featured a lavish party. He'd been reminded about his own invitation, which he'd put off responding to.

"It's only a drop-in. You could go in, make sure Cosette sees you there and then leave. Or, simply don't go at all. Case closed," said Myrtle. "You're a grown man. Since you're in your sixties, you're *very* grown up, actually. You don't have to go anywhere you don't want to go."

Miles traced a finger over the checked tablecloth covering Myrtle's kitchen table. "I've gotten tons of invitations from Cosette to parties and have turned so many of them down that I don't think I have it in me to turn down another single one."

"Why haven't you wanted to go to any of them?"

Miles colored. "Cosette is a terrible flirt. I never know what to make of it. And her husband is always *right there* while she's flirting."

"That goes to show that she means nothing at all by it. It's tacky, but it's simply the way she operates. Even Lucas thinks nothing of it." Myrtle shrugged.

"Maybe so, but it makes me uncomfortable. Not only that, but she invites some of her widowed friends over and it's obvious she's trying to match-make." Miles shifted in his seat.

"That's because you're such an impressive specimen," explained Myrtle, grinning mischievously at him. "You're a sophisticated guy from Atlanta who's gracing us with your retirement in tiny Bradley, North Carolina. You're a former professional—a successful architect…."

"Engineer," corrected Miles glumly.

"Whatever. The point is that you're very eligible to the biddies around here. Besides…you can still drive."

Miles sighed again. "I wish you'd stop bringing that up as a reason for my desirability. It's quite deflating to my ego."

"Think what people will say about me," said Myrtle. "They'll call me a coyote."

Miles thought this over. "I'm stumped. What's a coyote?"

"One of those women who goes out with much younger men. You're about twenty years younger, you know," said Myrtle.

"I believe you mean a *cougar*, not a coyote." He paused. "So will you go with me?"

"To protect you from the flirting hordes? Oh, I suppose so. I can appear quite threatening, I'm sure. I'm six feet tall and I wield a cane. Besides, I certainly don't have anything else to do tonight." Myrtle stared morosely at Miles.

"Thanks."

"But you owe me one," said Myrtle. "I don't like Cosette Whitlow one bit. She's extremely annoying. Every time she sees Red, she tells him how wonderful the Greener Pastures Retirement Home is and how much her addled mother *loves* being there. She brags on her toddler grandson as if he's a genius of some kind. I ordinarily avoid her like the plague." Her eyes scanned her kitchen cabinets. "Now I have to figure out what to bring to the drop-in. Maybe a dip of some kind."

Miles hastily said, "You really don't have to do that, Myrtle. You're already doing me a favor by coming. I'll bring a bottle of wine from the both of us and we'll count ourselves done."

"I could even bring something hot. I had some delicious stuffed mushrooms at Marybelle Stuart's house recently," said Myrtle.

"How about something simple, like a cheese tray?"

Myrtle said, "Anyone would think that you don't like my cooking, Miles!"

Miles pressed his lips shut as if to force some words back in. He was probably remembering that he needed to be on Myrtle's good side. "It's just that I don't want you to bother, that's all." There was a tap at Myrtle's front door and Miles said, "I've got to go, Myrtle. I'll answer that for you on my way out. See you around six-thirty."

He looked out the front window. "It's Red," he said and opened the door for Myrtle's son. Red gave Miles a cheerful greeting along with a goodbye as he saw he was leaving. Then Red grinned at his mother, who was walking into the living room to join him. The red hair that had given Red his nickname was turning gray and he was now in his mid-forties. He spent his days policing the small town of Bradley as its chief of police. And he spent his off-hours trying to keep

Myrtle in line. He was convinced that when Myrtle was bored, trouble soon followed.

Sure enough, he had plans for her free time. He was carrying knitting needles and a bag of yarn. Myrtle looked at them distastefully. "Where on earth did those things come from, Red?"

He sighed. "From Elaine. She's planning on bringing more over to you later."

Myrtle blinked at him. "I don't believe you. Your wife knows good and well that I'm no knitter."

"She knows that you know *how* to knit, though. And she's got a friend who is teaching her how to knit. Apparently, it's supposed to be very relaxing," said Red with a shrug as he plopped down across from his mother in the living room. It must be getting hot outside since beads of perspiration dotted his forehead, despite the fact that he'd only had to walk across the street to get to Myrtle's. Her small living room, which she preferred to think of as cozy, suddenly seemed cramped.

"Did you come straight here?" asked Myrtle frowning. "If you're that hot from just walking across the street, then there's no way I'm going out today."

Red paused as if weighing his options. He must be tempted to say that it was too hot for Myrtle outside…then he'd know she'd stay in and out of trouble. But he apparently decided to give her the truth. "I didn't come straight here, no, although it's plenty hot outside. Work has been busy lately. All kinds of mischief going on."

Myrtle's ears perked up. Busy days at the police department could make for interesting listening. "Mischief? What sort of mischief?" Maybe it had something to do with the fascinating saga down the street.

"Old Miz Marlson has been upset about clothes being stolen off her clothesline. She's been calling me up about every couple of hours to ask if I've caught the perpetrators." On cue, Red's cell phone rang. He took it off its holster and glumly surveyed it. "Yep. It's Miz Marlson."

Red took a deep breath and answered. "Miz Marlson? Yes. I'm working on it right now, that's right. I'm asking my mother if she's seen anybody suspicious lurking on the street." He rolled his eyes at Myrtle. "Mama? Have you seen anybody strange?"

"Erma Sherman is strange," muttered Myrtle, shuddering at the thought of her detested next-door-neighbor.

Red ignored her and said, "No, Miz Marlson, Mama hasn't noticed anybody. I'll keep investigating. We'll find the guy—don't you worry. Mmm-hmm." He hung up and sighed. "I do love small towns. I really do. I should be thanking my lucky stars every day that I'm in Bradley, North Carolina, worrying about stolen clothes and linens and not graffiti, murder, and mayhem."

Myrtle said, "If Mary Marlson had anything stolen from her, then I'm a monkey's uncle. She's probably stuck those clothes away in her closet and has forgotten she's done it."

"Oh," said Red, sounding startled. "Does she have Alzheimer's? No one bothered to tell me that. That's exactly the kind of thing I like to know so that I can keep an eye out for them and make sure they're safe."

"No. Just plain old absentmindedness. She was the same way when she was a girl," said Myrtle. "Told me I'd taken her favorite marble. Mary went on and on about it, the crazy thing. Later, I noticed her dress pocket appeared to have a small lump, and there was the marble. You should go visit her and have her check her closet for that stuff."

Red's voice was thoughtful now, "All right, Mama. Good idea."

"Now that I've saved you from a fruitless search for Mary Marlson's cotton dresses, why don't you give me the *real* scoop from around town? You've got to be able to do better than the Clothesline Capers," said Myrtle.

"Let's see," Red wrinkled his brow. "Not a whole lot, no. Jim Weller cussed out Tony Pearson at the barber shop. Something about mechanical incompetence. Launched himself at Tony and I had to step in. I was there getting a trim."

"Mechanical incompetence? Is that like medical incompetence?"

"I guess. Tony is a car mechanic and Jim thought Tony did more harm than good under the hood and now Jim has some expensive repairs. I calmed Jim down and helped mediate the dispute." Red shrugged.

"Being a small town cop isn't as boring as people think," said Myrtle.

"You got that right." Red stretched and stood up. "Time for me to head on out. I've still got to deal with Miz Marlson."

"Can you come back over later in the afternoon and take me to the grocery store?" Myrtle didn't have a car anymore, although she was very proud that she still had a license. "I'd ordinarily walk there, but I do have a gallon of milk to get this time. And I must pick up something to bring to Cosette Whitlow's drop-in tonight." Red frowned at her and she sighed. "Miles is making me go."

Red said, "Ah, Miles is behind it. I couldn't imagine you going there on your own. Weren't you complaining about her the other day—that you keep running into Cosette? I can't figure out where your path and Cosette's would ever cross."

"Everywhere. She's omnipresent like a malevolent spirit. Apparently, she's involved in every activity the town of Bradley has to offer. And either I *happen* to run into her all the time at the library, the post office, the drug store, and the grocery store, or else she's following me," said Myrtle.

"Hmm," said Red.

Myrtle narrowed her eyes. Usually when he said *hmm*, he was tuning her out. "And she has the audacity to take on a French name in Bradley, North Carolina. I'll eat my hat if that woman was born a Cosette. I'm thinking she was a Mary Elizabeth or a Darla Leigh or a Peggy Jo."

Red looked to the heavens in supplication to the gods.

"And she brags on her grandson constantly. Noah. The one who's Jack's age."

Jack was Red and Elaine's son. "What kinds of things was she saying about Noah?" asked Red curiously.

"Oh, you know. Little Noah can read all the board books in his house. Little Noah can count to a thousand. Little Noah memorized the Pythagorean Theorem. That sort of thing. It's most vexing. Especially since we know that Jack is much more advanced than Noah is. More advanced than *any* child in Bradley."

"Anything else?" asked Red. "You may as well get it all out of your system now."

"She's all prickly and pointy. Sharp features, sharp chin, bony elbows and knees. Sharp tongue, too—she's always fussing at her poor husband. He's still got quite a limp from his knee surgery, but that doesn't stop her from running him ragged. Yes, sharp all over. When I look at her, I think *ouch*."

Red chuckled. "If you say so, Mama. All right, I'm heading out the door." His glance fell on the knitting needles and bag of yarn. "Enjoy your knitting."

Myrtle eyed the bag with distaste. "I certainly won't. Much as I love Elaine, I'll be handing over this knitting stuff as soon as I see her. She knows me better than that."

"Elaine probably thought it was an activity that y'all could do together. Granny knitted, as I recall, and she had you knitting right alongside her," said Red mildly.

"Many years ago," said Myrtle with a sigh. She paused. "Knitting makes me feel old. It made me feel old when I was twenty and doing it."

"It's supposed to be relaxing," offered Red.

"It stresses me out."

"It couldn't possibly," said Red stoutly. "Everyone says it's relaxing."

"Maybe everyone doesn't end up with whole rows out of place. Or maybe they don't end up with really tight stitches."

"Just think, Mama: knitting will provide you with an excellent cover. Folks will be lulled into a false sense of security. They'll see an old lady in her eighties innocuously knitting away, and they'll spill all kinds of secrets. Think of all the undercover snooping you can do. I know you like to snoop."

"Well, I like to snoop more than I like to knit, that's for sure." She paused. "Is Elaine *good* at knitting?"

Red rolled his eyes and he and his mother shared a look of rare solidarity.

"I suppose you and I will be wearing dreadful knitted hats and scarves this winter," said Myrtle with a shudder.

"I'm praying for another warm winter," said Red fervently as he walked out the door.

Chapter Two

That afternoon at the grocery store, Myrtle once again ran into Cosette Whitlow. There she was, right in the dairy section, with her stodgy husband Lucas at her beck and call, as usual.

Red had driven her to the store, as promised. He said under his breath, "Here's Cosette now. Isn't she the focus of your current fascination?"

"Fascination and repulsion, all at once," muttered Myrtle. She reached for a bag of dog food.

"Here, I'll get that," said Red briskly. "It must weigh twenty pounds, Mama. Wait. You have a *cat*, not a dog."

"I'm donating dog food to the Bradley Animal Shelter. I read in the paper that they were running low."

"Okay. Well, remind me and I'll take it by while I'm on patrol. We don't need you lugging twenty pounds of dog food on foot." He glanced up. "Looks like Cosette is coming over," he muttered.

"Oh *hel*-lo, Miss Myrtle! Getting your pantry stocked up?" asked Cosette with a condescending smile on her face and the kind of tone reserved for small children or imbecilic pets.

Myrtle gave her a tight smile in return. "That's right. And while you're here, I wanted to let you know that I'm coming to your party tonight. I'm going with Miles."

"Isn't that *won*derful?" sang out Cosette, giving a broad wink to Red. "I simply love it when our senior citizens still enjoy a love life. It's so very important, don't you think, Lucas?"

Lucas quickly nodded, beaming at them.

"Vital, I think," said Red, nodding and patting his mother on the back. "Helps them live longer, better, more meaningful lives." His lips twitched as if longing to break into a grin.

"Miles and I are *not* having a relationship as you well know, Red Clover," snapped Myrtle.

"That's something else I admire about your mother," said Cosette, blinking flirtatiously at Red. "She's just so plucky! Cute and plucky!"

Myrtle glared at her and Red made a sneezing sound that Myrtle guessed was his attempt at holding back a laugh. It was most annoying when people treated the elderly as if they were children. Myrtle had never been cute. And she preferred *capable* or *courageous* to *plucky*.

Myrtle smiled through gritted teeth. She would try to be patient. "How funny to see you and Lucas here, Cosette. I see you everywhere I go, I think. You must be the busiest woman in Bradley."

Lucas said shyly, "She is. Excuse my bragging, but Bradley couldn't do without her. She's in charge of the Women's Club, the Bradley Garden Club, the historical society, and volunteers for several committees at church. That doesn't include all the things she does at the house—Cosette keeps the house meticulously clean, and cooks like a professional chef." He gazed proudly at his wife.

Cosette simpered in response, "Are you still active around town, Miss Myrtle?"

Myrtle shrugged. "I write a column for the *Bradley Bugle*. And I do special investigative reports for them sometimes, too."

Cosette was momentarily distracted as Lucas pulled a bag of chips from a nearby end cap. She said harshly, "Lucas—put that back. You've got to lose weight."

She quickly turned back to Myrtle. "You write stories for the paper? Isn't that sweet!" beamed Cosette. "I should recruit you for some of the organizations that I'm heading up. You could do some real good in this town, you know."

Myrtle frowned at her. "I've already done plenty of good. And I've been in all those clubs, off and on, for about sixty years." Cosette appeared to be opening her mouth to try and enlist Myrtle again so Myrtle quickly said, "Well, if you'll excuse me, I have some shopping to do." She hurried toward the milk.

She could still plainly hear Cosette Whitlow talking to Red in a hushed voice. It was amazing the things people would whisper in Myrtle's presence because they assumed she was going deaf. It was an incorrect and potentially hazardous assumption to make.

Cosette said, "I know your mother is a handful. But I've got my own dear mother in Greener Pastures Retirement Home and it has been a real blessing. She'll simply love it. They have darling activities—themed Bingo nights, variety shows, and sittercise for the wheelchair bound. And now Mother isn't calling me up all the time and asking me to change her light bulbs. They take care of her there. It's just a lovely, lovely place for our precious older adults."

Myrtle's back stiffened as she listened. The gall of the woman. Why didn't it surprise her that she'd stuck her mother in a retirement home when she got on her nerves?

"Thanks for the recommendation, Cosette. I've been considering Greener Pastures for years. Although I have a feeling that Mama isn't quite ready to transition there yet," said Red politely. Myrtle turned to shoot him a murderous look and Red grinned at her.

"You don't have to wait for it to be her idea. Do you know what I'd do, Red? I'd march straight out to the Greener Pastures Retirement Home right now and I'd beg them to take your Mama."

Red's voice sounded doubtful. "Well… Mama isn't real keen on Greener Pastures. She still likes to putter around in her house and yard an awful lot."

"Putter? Fall down is more likely. I've seen her balance on that cane of hers...very precarious she is too. Believe me, once she gets used to it out there, she'll love it. I volunteer there all the time and it's just a *lovely* community."

Myrtle was tired of pretending that she couldn't hear them. "Maybe I'll go there…once I get old."

"Well, anytime you change your mind, sweetie," said Cosette in a louder voice to Myrtle, "you let me know. I can drive you there for the day and my precious Mama can show you around."

Cosette's voice dripped with sugar until she abruptly barked at her husband, "Lucas! What's this nonsense that you've put in the cart? Put it back. We don't need that. What were you thinking?" Her berating of poor Lucas continued as they wheeled their shopping buggy out of sight.

Myrtle hadn't been particularly creative with the hors d'oeuvre she brought to Cosette's house. It was merely a spinach and artichoke dip with crackers alongside. She'd seen Miles eye it with suspicion, however, as they walked up Cosette's driveway. "It's a basic dip, Miles. It's not going to leap out to poison you."

"Won't it?" asked Miles. "I've eaten your cooking before, remember?"

"That's rude. Besides, you really can't mess up spinach and artichoke dip," said Myrtle with a sniff.

"Can't you?" asked Miles. He didn't sound at all convinced.

"Now don't hang all over me at this party," said Myrtle. "For some reason, Cosette seems to think we're an item."

"I'll try to restrain myself," said Miles, rolling his eyes. "That's all I need."

Myrtle squinted at Miles to see if he was being ugly and stumbled, catching herself with her cane and nearly dropping the platter she'd been determined to carry herself.

"Here, give me that," said Miles, removing the platter from her hand. "For heaven's sake."

Since they'd carefully devised not to be the first guests on the scene, there were plenty of other people there. Most of the neighbors who lived on their street seemed to be in attendance—including Erma, Myrtle was sorry to note—as well as couples from the church and other organizations. It was a full house.

Miles was still awkwardly clutching both Myrtle's platter and the bottle of wine that he'd brought. "Here, we should put those things down somewhere," said Myrtle loudly over the din of conversations and laughter.

"The food seems to be laid out over there," said Miles, nodding his head over at the dining room where trays of food were visible on the table and sideboard.

Myrtle scanned the crowd. The coast was clear. No annoying Cosette. She might be in the kitchen, getting drinks or more food. "I think there's room for my spinach and artichoke dip, but let's put your wine in the kitchen. There isn't enough room for it in the dining room." Perhaps she could sneak in and deposit it without Cosette's cloying comments about *precious older adults*.

Miles frowned at her. "Not enough room for a small bottle, but enough room for a dip platter?"

But Myrtle was already making room for her hors d'oeuvres, pushing aside a tray of Buffalo wings and dressing. "There." She wove her way through the crowd of people toward the kitchen and Miles slowly followed her.

The house was a typical three-bedroom ranch, like the other homes on their street. But the inside was quite lavishly decorated. It wasn't only that the furniture looked both very fine and brand-new, but that the house itself had been renovated. There were parquet floors (what Myrtle could see of the floors, anyway, with so many people there) and crown molding. And, once she finally reached the kitchen, she could see it was filled with granite countertops and stainless steel appliances. A lot of money had been poured into this fairly simple house.

As feared, Cosette was in the kitchen, but she appeared to be engaged in an argument with someone on her phone. This provided perfect cover for Myrtle to quickly put down the wine. She had her back toward them, and didn't see as they entered the room.

Miles immediately started backing away. "Myrtle," he hissed. "Come on. Let's put the wine down in the dining room."

"The least you could do is come over here, Joan," said Cosette in a shrewish voice that sounded nothing like the saccharine tones that she always bestowed on Myrtle. "I'm your mother and I don't ask for much." She paused. "No, I don't! I brought you up with the finest education, gave you a debut, and made sure you had every advantage, young lady. How have you repaid me? By marrying a plumber and then divorcing him a couple of months before your baby was due. The least, the very least I expect from you, is to make an appearance when I have a soiree." She abruptly hung up and threw her cell phone across the kitchen.

This time when Miles motioned desperately to her to leave, Myrtle did.

"Did you understand all of that?" asked Miles as they headed back into the noisy dining room. "It sounded like the storyline on one of your soaps."

"My soap would know better than to run a tired plot like that," said Myrtle. "And yes, I did understand it. I forget that you're a relative newcomer to Bradley. Cosette has always thrown lavish parties. She has doted on her daughter ever since she was a baby—buying her the most ridiculously expensive baby clothes, sending her off to private school, throwing a huge sweet-sixteen party for her," explained Myrtle.

Someone jostled Miles's arm on their way to the chicken wings and he grimaced. "Where did Cosette get the money for that kind of stuff? It seems like they live in a pretty modest house. Isn't Lucas an accountant or something?" He put a couple of deviled eggs and some spicy cheese straws on a plate.

Myrtle had already fixed herself some crackers with a pepper jelly and cream cheese spread. She munched for a moment, and then said, "That's right. I always wondered about the money, but then they'd start living their usual, modest lives again. But lately, Cosette seems like she's been really spending with a vengeance. Renovations to the house, cruises abroad. I guess the money must be burning a hole in her pocket again. Now she's giving Joan a guilt trip about not being here."

"What's Joan like?" asked Miles. "I don't think I've ever met her." He made a small plate of mini ham biscuits and he and Myrtle shared them.

"You probably wouldn't have had the opportunity to. She lives on the other side of Bradley, for one. And she has Noah—Cosette's grandson. I think whenever she goes anywhere, she's going to things that other young mothers would go to. She's nothing at all like her mother. She's a bit chubby, has mousy-hair, is inordinately fond of workout clothing for someone who clearly doesn't work out, and wears thick glasses." She heard the front door and frowned.

"Can anyone else fit into this house? I can't imagine what the fire marshal would say." She squinted. "Is that Sybil? And Felix. Felix looks rather unhappy." Sybil spotted them and waved, long brown hair swishing. Everything on her swished, actually—she wore a ruffled peasant dress, as usual, with swinging hoop earrings that were large enough to brush her shoulder.

"Doesn't Felix always look unhappy?" asked Miles.

"As a matter of fact, he does," mused Myrtle. "Always looks like he's suffering from a dire case of indigestion or something." The dour Felix was scanning the room as if looking for someone. He appeared to have no interest in sticking close to Sybil. He absently straightened his already-straight bow tie.

Myrtle and Miles nibbled poppy seed ham biscuits and watched as Sybil quickly came toward them and put down a plate of vegetables and dip in the dining room. "Hi, Miss Myrtle and Miles!" she sang out loudly. Myrtle had the distinct impression that Sybil might have had more than one glass of wine before coming here. She bestowed an exuberant kiss on Myrtle's cheek, although she barely knew the woman. "So good to see y'all. What do you think of the new book club selection so far? I *love* it! I'm almost done reading." She grinned at them—white teeth showing in a tanned face.

Myrtle wasn't sure she had it in her to summon up any kind words regarding the book club selection and her mother had always taught her that if she didn't have anything nice to say, not to say anything at all. It was a rule that she'd found very difficult to abide by (*impossible* to abide by most of the time), but now she bit her tongue and watched with relief as Miles chimed in to answer the question.

"*Penelope's Problem*?" asked Miles.

Myrtle was astounded that he was able to pull up that ridiculous title from the depths of his brain. He must have a Rolodex in his head.

"Was that your book pick?" Miles delicately asked Sybil.

She beamed at him. "It sure was. Aren't you absolutely loving it?"

Myrtle could tell by the faint color on Miles' face both that he hadn't read it and that he was about to fib. "It's good. Very good. Yes, that Penelope really does have a problem. It's a problem all right."

Myrtle toyed with the idea of not rescuing him, but then decided it made her feel too awkward to watch Miles stumble through his fake book review. "I'm sure it's fine, Sybil, but I always hold out hope that our book club might start reading actual *literature*. I'm not sure what Penelope's problem is, but I'm sure it can't compete with Oliver Twist's, for instance."

Sybil looked puzzled. "Is Oliver in book club? I'm trying to learn everybody's name, since I'm sort of new in town still. I thought Miles was the only man in our club."

Myrtle realized with dawning horror that Sybil didn't recognize a Charles Dickens title when she heard one. She started spluttering.

Miles smoothly stepped in, "Anyway, it's nice to see you here, Sybil. I don't ever really get a chance to talk to you much in book club."

Sybil gave him a sly look and giggled. "That's because you're fending off all the widows. Poor guy. The only rooster in the hen house."

"Now you're embarrassing him, Sybil," said Myrtle. "Miles always thinks he's surrounded by book club members because of his expert analysis of each month's book." She glanced around them, which was hard to do with the crowd of people. "Speaking of surrounded, what happened to Felix? I thought he came in with you."

Sybil pouted. "He did come in with me. You'd think he'd try to stay with me, wouldn't you? As a couple? Most of the couples I know talk to other guests together."

She turned her head, searching the crowd. "Where did Felix run off to?" she asked in a fretful tone. "Usually he ends up somewhere close to the food."

Cosette's husband, Lucas, walked into the dining room looking distracted. He picked up a wine glass and poured himself a large glass of chardonnay. "Lucas," asked Sybil, "have you seen Felix?"

He started at the question, sloshing his wine so that some spilled out onto his button-down shirt. He dabbed at it, not meeting Sybil's eyes. "I believe I saw him in the kitchen," he said.

Myrtle and Miles exchanged a look.

"Thanks," said Sybil. She started heading toward the kitchen, and then stopped. "You know, I believe I'll have a glass of wine, myself." She strode to the sideboard and poured herself a large glass of red wine, and then drank large gulps of it as she walked out of the room.

"I don't think she needs any more wine," said Miles, raising his eyebrows.

Lucas drank his chardonnay quickly, and then poured himself another as guests came up to greet him.

"Clearly, you haven't read *Penelope's Problem*," said Myrtle.

"Of course not. And don't tell me that *you've* read it. I won't believe you."

"I haven't read it," said Myrtle, shuddering.

"It's not *that* bad. I did start it. Well, I started skimming it. It had some very interesting elements to it, actually. It's about a woman trying to discover who she really is during her midlife…."

"Oh please. As if we haven't read *that* plot before. So she goes to Italy and meets a chef and eats fabulous food and discovers life's meaning in the Tuscan sunshine." Myrtle made a raspberry to indicate what she thought of that plotline. She was tiring of the subject. "You know what I'd like, Miles? A glass of water. But I believe I'll have to go into the kitchen for that, since there are no water pitchers that I can see."

Miles gave her a weary look. "I may as well give in. You want to see what's going on between Felix, Cosette, and Sybil. There's no use in fighting it, I suppose."

"None at all," said Myrtle, already heading toward the kitchen.

Chapter Three

They peered around the door and spotted Felix, Sybil, and Cosette staring silently at each other. The water was instantly forgotten and Myrtle and Miles hovered in the kitchen door, not entering the room. What was playing out was as familiar to Myrtle as old storylines on her soap opera.

"I knew it!" Sybil was hissing, with the same over-the-top melodrama employed by Myrtle's soap.

Felix said coldly, "Get ahold of yourself, Sybil. You're misreading the whole situation."

"No you're not," said Cosette quickly, with a smirk at Sybil.

Sybil gave a half-sob. "You'll be sorry, Cosette," she hollered as she bolted for the kitchen door, pushing past Myrtle and Miles on the way out.

Felix and Cosette suddenly noticed Miles and Myrtle standing there. "Um. Water?" asked Myrtle.

Felix muttered something that sounded suspiciously like *snoopy old woman* before striding out of the room.

Miles glared at Myrtle and was just opening his mouth, probably to say something placating to Cosette, who seemed on the verge of explosion, when a toddler ran into the kitchen.

"Noah!" said Cosette, frowning down at the child as if he'd grown horns. Her daughter, Joan, came into the kitchen next. Cosette proceeded to ignore Myrtle and Miles, and Joan did too. "I didn't tell you to bring the baby to the drop-in, Joan. Whatever are you thinking?"

Joan said icily, "I'm thinking that I have no one to watch Noah for me and that you have no right throwing a guilt trip at me for not being here. But since it's so important to you, I'm here. With Noah."

"Well, Noah is an extremely advanced boy, but I don't think even *he* belongs at a party for grownups. We'll bore him to tears." Cosette stood, staring at the baby as he took some pots and pans out of the cabinet and started banging on them with a spatula. "I know what we'll do. Constance Walker is here with her teenage daughter. I'll ask Ginny if she can take Noah into my bedroom to play."

Without asking, she strode out. Joan's face was strained and splotched with red as she watched her mother leave with Noah firmly in tow. She didn't seem dressed for a party in any way. She wore navy-blue sweatpants and a stained tee shirt and hadn't even appeared to have brushed her mousy brown hair.

"I've had it with her," she muttered to herself. "I'm done. Done!"

Joan barely glanced at Myrtle or Miles on the way out.

"I have to admit," Myrtle said slowly, "that although I've heard the elderly are frequently treated as if they are invisible, I've never actually experienced it to this degree."

"They were all too caught up in their drama to spare us a glance," said Miles, looking green around the edges.

Myrtle studied him. "I know you don't like conflict, but try to buck up. It's all over now. It was fairly eye-opening; although I'm not sure I understood all of what was going on."

"Are you sure it's over?" asked Miles doubtfully. "It doesn't seem that way to me. It seems like they are just getting geared up."

"I think we'll find that everything will settle down now that Cosette's grandson is on the scene. Funny how a child can make adults act more mature," said Myrtle.

"Except for the fact that she relegated him to her bedroom with a sitter. It doesn't sound like he's going to have much of a chance to make the adults cool down."

Myrtle said, "Let's find out how things are going out there."

She turned to exit the kitchen and Miles stopped her. "Let's get you a glass of water, since that was your excuse for coming into the kitchen to start with."

"I guess I should," said Myrtle with a sigh. "Although I still don't think they were paying any attention to me or my excuse at all."

With glass in hand, they walked back out to join the rest of the party. "It seems to me that a few people have already left," said Myrtle. She raised her eyebrows. "But Sybil is still here."

"She probably thought that if she left too early, people might suspect a scene," said Miles with a small shrug. "Do you think Felix left?" asked Miles.

"I doubt Felix cares if he makes a scene or not," said Myrtle. "I don't see him. Maybe he decided to leave."

"Lucas seems to be stepping into the hosting duties," said Miles thoughtfully.

"I guess Cosette must have trained him well," said Myrtle. Lucas was busily clearing away empty plates and glasses and returning with a tray of mini quiches and pickled shrimp before disappearing again. His limp seemed a bit more pronounced with all the activity.

"I don't see Joan, do you?" asked Myrtle, peering around the crowded living room and dining room.

"She's probably making sure her child is all right," said Miles with a snort. "It didn't sound like she'd even heard of the babysitter that Cosette was putting Noah with." He shifted restlessly. "Did you get all your snooping out of your system?" he asked rather plaintively. "I'm ready to get out of here. I think Cosette registered my attendance, even as preoccupied as she was. Actually, I was ready to leave as soon as we arrived."

"Oh, I suppose so. You're no fun, Miles. What else do you have to do tonight? Read *Penelope's Promise?*"

"I'm sure I can think of something more entertaining than being here. Folding laundry holds more appeal, as a matter of fact," said Miles.

Myrtle heard a familiar voice behind her. She turned to see Sloan Jones talking loudly to someone across from him. Sloan was the editor at the *Bradley Bugle* and Myrtle wrote a weekly helpful hints column for him, although she'd much rather be writing an investigative report or following a big story for the paper. Sloan had his back to her.

"That's right," Sloan was saying loudly over the noise from the party. "I felt like we needed a fresh voice in the newsroom. I've been writing stories for the paper for forever, it seems like. And poor Miss Myrtle…" He chuckled. "She's not exactly on the cutting edge of journalism. So I've got this intern for a while. We'll see how she does. I'm excited about it."

Myrtle turned back at Miles who was looking sympathetically at her. "All right, I'm ready to go now. Let's go that way so that you-know-who doesn't realize I was listening to him."

"Let's find Cosette and thank her and get out of here," agreed Miles.

"You're such a stickler for observing the proprieties," murmured Myrtle. "Let's see. I guess she's back in the kitchen again. I haven't seen her out here or in the dining room and Lucas has taken over all the hosting duties."

They walked back to the kitchen and looked inside. Lucas was busily stirring another pitcher of sweet tea. "Can I help you with anything?" he asked politely, perspiration dotting his forehead.

"No, we're just looking for Cosette to thank her and tell her bye," said Myrtle.

Miles quickly added, "But since we can't seem to locate her, we'll thank you, instead, for our very pleasant evening." He took Myrtle by the arm to pull her gently back to the kitchen door.

Lucas looked startled. "You haven't seen Cosette? I mean, I haven't seen her either, but I assumed she was deep in conversation with somebody at the party…that's why I jumped in to help with the food." He absently put down the tea pitcher, nearly dropping it on the floor in the process. "Maybe we should look for her."

Miles sighed and Myrtle said quickly, "I think we should. Although she might very well be in your bedroom with Noah. You saw that your grandson was here, didn't you?"

This information seemed to be a surprise to Lucas, too. "Noah? How did he get here? I haven't seen Joan."

"Joan is here somewhere—I think. At any rate, we saw Joan arrive with Noah, but we haven't seen her for a while. Cosette found a teenager to look after Noah," said Myrtle. Lucas was truly looking puzzled and she said quickly, "Let's look around for both of them."

The first place they checked was the master bedroom. A bored-looking teen gave them a quick smile as they entered. Toddler Noah was playing with a coloring book—in theory, anyway. He seemed to be tasting all the different colors of crayons. There was no sight of Cosette or Joan and the teenager hadn't seen either one since she'd been asked by Cosette to watch Noah.

As they left the room, Myrtle muttered to Miles. "Genius. Right. He's busy eating his crayons"

"Is that still bothering you?" said Miles.

"It is. Jack is just as smart as little Noah and I don't feel the need to go blabbing around town about his brilliance. Cosette is so—"

"Annoying," said Miles.

Annoying—and missing. They looked for her in the crowded living room, the dining room, and even knocked on the hall bathroom to make sure she wasn't in there. Everyone had seen her, but no one had seen her recently.

Lucas's face appeared strained. They'd retreated back to the kitchen to talk, since they could barely hear each other in the other rooms. "Where could she have gone? And during a drop-in? That's not like her. She's always a good hostess."

Myrtle said, "The only place we haven't checked is outside. She's clearly not inside."

"Why on earth would she go outside? I mean—she's an outdoor person, but why now?" He gave a rough laugh. "I don't go outside at all myself anymore—gardening never caught on for me."

"Who knows?" asked Myrtle impatiently. "But we should check. And we should make sure her car is here, too."

"I can't imagine Cosette driving away from a *party*," said Lucas.

"Maybe she suddenly realized y'all were out of ice or something," said Miles. "It happens."

They walked out the kitchen door onto the back porch and into the attached garage. Cosette's sedan was still there. "I didn't think she would leave," said Lucas. "But where is she?"

"Can you turn on any lights that will shine in the backyard?" asked Myrtle. "It's the only place we haven't checked." She gripped her cane. She *was* fairly sturdy on her feet, really. Just not on soil.

Lucas obediently stepped into the kitchen and flipped some switches, and lights came on at the back corners of the ranch house and outside the back porch. Myrtle peered into the darkness. There was a dark lump on the ground near the line of trees leading down to the lake.

Myrtle gripped her cane and opened the screen door, moving carefully into the yard. "Do y'all see something there? On the ground…near the woods?"

Lucas froze in place as Myrtle and Miles hurried forward.

It was Cosette, sprawled face-first on the damp ground. A bloody croquet mallet lay next to her.

Chapter Four

Lucas Whitlow seemed intent on leaping across the yard and completely mucking up the crime scene.

Fortunately, Miles was able to hold his arm and stop him. "Lucas, there's nothing you can do now. I'm so sorry. Let's go inside and call the police right away. We need to find out who did this, and treading into the crime scene won't help."

The poor man was completely devastated, trembling all over. "Are you sure? There's no doubt.... I didn't even know we owned a croquet set. I never go out into the yard, you see. There's nothing we can do...?" He looked as if he might become ill.

"I'm afraid not," said Myrtle shaking her head and gently motioning Lucas back toward the screened porch. "Why don't you head inside with Miles while I call Red?"

Miles carefully led Lucas back into the house while Myrtle drew closer to the body on the ground. She wouldn't disturb the crime scene, but she'd take a couple of pictures of it for future reference. Red and the state police could be stingy with their information.

Myrtle studied the area. She didn't see any footprints or any obvious clues. It certainly didn't appear that Cosette had put up any kind of a fight against her murderer—there were no cuts or injuries on Cosette besides the fatal blow with the mallet. There was no torn clothing. She must have come outside to speak with someone privately. The party had been so loud that the only quiet place had been the kitchen, and she couldn't count on even that being private—Cosette had seen Miles and Myrtle tramping through to get water.

Cosette must have known her killer. Of course, in Bradley this wasn't exactly outside the realm of possibility.

Everyone in the town knew each other---by sight, anyway. So maybe it was more as if Cosette knew her killer and *trusted* him.

Myrtle punched in Red's number on her phone.

"Mama?" asked Red. "Is everything all right?"

"Not exactly, no. I'm at Cosette's drop-in…."

Red groaned. "Oh, Mama. You're not going to ask me to make an appearance there, are you? I'm already settled in for the night with my TV show. You couldn't get me to Cosette and Lucas's party with a cattle prod."

"Well, I'd better get out my cattle prod. Cosette is dead. She was murdered out in the yard, and Miles, Lucas, and I just discovered her."

This time instead of a groan, there was a muttered oath. "All right, I'm coming. Let me call the state police to report it and pull my uniform back on. She was definitely murdered?"

"No question about it. She could hardly have hit herself on the head with a croquet mallet," said Myrtle.

"Croquet mallet?" She heard Red's heavy sigh on the other end of the phone. "I never cared for Cosette much, but she certainly didn't deserve that. All right, I'm on my way. Keep everybody away from the body—that goes for you too, Mama."

"I wouldn't dream of interfering with a crime scene," said Myrtle with a sniff. She hung up and waited to fend off the inevitable hoard of curious partygoers.

And it didn't happen. Myrtle raised her eyebrows. Miles must be corralling the distraught Lucas in the kitchen. He always did have a good head on his shoulders.

In fact, the party's awareness of their hostess's body in the backyard didn't occur until Red's police car showed up at the front of the house. He didn't bother walking through the house, choosing instead to come straight around the house to the back. That was when several of the guests decided to find out where he was going.

The next thing Myrtle knew, there was a throng of guests on the back porch, murmuring to each other in horror.

Red, who was still talking to the state police on his phone, turned and said, "Everyone please stay inside the house. No one should leave until I've had the opportunity to speak to them." He said to Myrtle, "Mama, please back up and get on the back porch or go inside. Take a seat and I'll question you in a little bit." She must have had a look of great consternation on her face, because he said more gently, "Why don't you tell everyone inside what's happened and make sure no one leaves."

Myrtle was always happier when she had a specific job to do. She carefully leaned on her cane as she walked back inside and positioned herself by the front door to make sure no one got past her. The only thing she didn't do was to tell everyone what had happened. Because Red had somehow forgotten that in a small town like Bradley, news of murder spread like wildfire.

Sure enough, within minutes, the raucous laughter had all quieted down into solemn murmurs as the guests tried to figure out what was going on. When they approached the door, Myrtle told them that Red had said that no one could leave until he'd spoken with everyone.

Miles came up to Myrtle, looking irritated, reaching for the front door handle. "Miles, Red said no one can leave yet."

He frowned at her. "Myrtle, I've got to get some air. It's getting too hot in here with all these bodies packed together."

"I'm not sure that *bodies* is the right word to use."

"Regardless. It's not like Red can't find me. I just want to get outside for a while," said Miles.

"How was Lucas doing?"

"About how you'd expect. He really seemed to love Cosette, so he's very broken up about this."

Myrtle said, "Where is he? Is he talking with Red?"

"No, I took him to their bedroom so that he could be away from everyone. The last I saw, he was playing with blocks with Noah and seemed to be trying really hard to hold himself together," said Miles. He pulled the door open. "Don't worry, I'll tell Red that I forced myself past you if he asks."

He stopped short as he was about to step through the door and made a face. Myrtle pivoted around to see what he was staring at. There was an overflowing bag of trash on the front porch, blocking the way. "I guess Lucas couldn't handle hosting duties so perfectly, after all."

It was taking a while for Red to interview everyone there.

"It's a large party. It might take a while," said Myrtle.

Miles had decided that perhaps he should stay at the drop-in after all. "I wouldn't think Red would have to question *everyone*, though. Wouldn't he immediately try to ascertain whether they'd seen or heard anything, then let them go?"

"Who knows?" said Myrtle gloomily. "He tries to keep me in the dark when it comes to his investigating techniques. I'm sure he'll get to us soon."

Miles deflated. Myrtle said, "Don't be tiresome, Miles. You're the one who wanted to come to this party.

"Yes, but I never thought I'd be stuck here all night."

"Come on, let's find ourselves a snack while we're waiting for Red," said Myrtle, pulling Miles by his sleeve.

Unfortunately, the food on the dining room table had been decimated. Except for Myrtle's spinach dip. "Well, at least the dip is left, Miles. It's barely been touched. Although the silly people ate all the crackers and left the dip!"

One of the guests overheard her and turned around, "Better keep away from that dip, Miss Myrtle. It's lethal. I don't know who brought it, but they went way overboard with the mayonnaise. The whole thing was mayonnaise, actually, with small bits of spinach in it. It was pretty sickening."

Myrtle frowned fiercely, but decided not to claim the dip as her own. Miles finally cracked his first smile of the evening.

And, after all of that, even the interview was cut and dried.

Red had claimed the kitchen as a temporary police station and listened carefully as Myrtle and Miles explained how they'd looked for Cosette to tell her goodbye and had finally resorted to looking in the backyard. "How long was it before you noticed that Cosette was missing?" he asked.

Miles and Myrtle stared at each other. "Maybe forty-five minutes?" guessed Myrtle. "The last we saw her, she was setting little Noah up with a babysitter. I don't think I saw her after that."

"And shortly afterward, Lucas stepped in with the hosting duties," said Miles. "So it wasn't very long."

"Did you notice if anyone was conspicuously absent?" asked Red, tilting his head to one side like he always did when he was intent on gathering information.

"Lots of nomadic, restless people at this drop-in," said Myrtle with a shrug. "They left the living room for the dining room, for the restroom, for the living room. I didn't bother tracking them."

"Did you see what happened to Joan, Cosette's daughter?" asked Red.

"I didn't see her," said Myrtle.

"I heard that Sybil Nelson seemed upset with Cosette. Do you know anything about that, Mama?" asked Red.

"Was she?" At least they had another lead to go on. This corroborated what they'd seen in the kitchen.

Red jotted down some notes in a small notebook he carried. "Okay. So you don't know anything about Sybil or Joan. And Lucas—Cosette's husband," he said, studying them carefully. "What do you remember of his movements?"

Myrtle pursed her lips in thought. "The husband is always the prime suspect, isn't he? Let's see. He was in and out an awful lot, wasn't he, Miles?"

Miles bobbed his head. "That's right. He was really working hard. Perspiring, actually, as he'd run in and out of the dining room, taking out empty plates and glasses and coming back for more. I remember that I felt guilty I wasn't helping him."

"So he was removing used dishes," said Red.

"And bringing out more food, too," said Myrtle. "There were these little sandwiches that everyone was gobbling up." She made a face. It was most irritating that her spinach dip hadn't been as popular as the crust-less sandwiches.

"In other words, he seemed very occupied and he always came right back into the dining room to get dirty plates or to bring fresh food," said Red. "There was no time for Lucas to have dodged out into the backyard to murder Cosette?"

Myrtle and Miles considered this. "Well, now, I wouldn't say that, either. Would you, Miles?" asked Myrtle.

"He wasn't *only* working. He was being a good host. Guests were talking to him and he was being friendly," said Miles. "It wasn't like he was only dashing back and forth to the kitchen."

"And I wasn't timing him," said Myrtle. "He might have gone to the kitchen and spent five minutes or ten minutes in there before returning to the dining room and I wouldn't have noticed it. If it had been longer than *that*, I probably would have. But it seems to me that it wouldn't have taken much time to run outside, bop Cosette over the head with a croquet mallet, and then quickly resume his hosting duties. He was already perspiring, as Miles said. No one would have thought anything of it."

Red made more notes in his notebook.

Myrtle frowned. "Don't you think, though, that whoever is responsible for this murder should have blood stains spattered on his or her top? Lucas is definitely wearing exactly the same shirt that he had on when we arrived."

"Unless he has several of the same shirt," pointed out Miles.

Myrtle glared at him. "Who on earth has a closet full of the same shirt?"

"I can think of several comic strip characters who must," said Red in a musing tone.

Miles said, "Sometimes, if I really like a shirt, I'll buy several of them. Simply because they're comfortable."

"Hmm. That actually makes a lot of sense," grunted Red.

Myrtle waved her cane at them to get their attention. "Enough! The point is that it's *unlikely* that Lucas changed clothes. Shouldn't he have blood on him if he did it?"

Red shook his head. "Not necessarily. The forensic team will come up with a report, but I'd say by looking at the scene, that any spattering would have gone away from the perpetrator instead of toward him." Red closed his notebook. "Okay, I guess that's it for now. I know where to find you if I have any other questions."

Would he? Myrtle intended to get to the bottom of this case herself. Good luck to Red if he tried to find her at home.

Myrtle was wide awake at two o'clock that morning. This happened all the time, but usually she'd fold some laundry or unload the dishwasher or clip coupons, or do something equally boring, and then go right back to sleep.

Tonight was different. Her mind was racing, returning to the moment she'd discovered Cosette in the backyard.

She hesitated just a moment before opening her front door. Her eyes fell on the knitting that Elaine had brought over. Then she snorted at the thought that had crossed her mind and quickly grabbed her cane and walked outside. Surely, Miles would be up too. He had insomnia as much as she did, and he'd had the same disturbing evening. Of course, he *had* been kind of grouchy, but he should have gotten over it by now. Myrtle continued down the sidewalk, thumping with her cane as she went.

There were no lights on that Myrtle could see, but she knew that Miles frequently preferred tossing and turning in bed to getting up. This was a mistake in Myrtle's eyes. She got lots done in the middle of the night. It was her most productive time, as a matter of fact.

She rang the bell and waited. Sometimes Miles even had coffee cups ready for them, and cookies and perked coffee. She smiled in anticipation.

The reality, when Miles finally opened the door, didn't match her hopes. No coffee cups, only a surly expression. He wore plaid pajamas with a navy bathrobe hastily tied over them. His iron-gray hair stood up on one side like a wing.

Myrtle blinked at him. "Gosh, Miles, you look terrible. What happened to you? Aren't you well?"

"Sleep happened to me. And not enough of it," said Miles with dignity, futilely trying to smooth down the errant hair.

He didn't seem to be in any hurry to invite her in, so Myrtle squeezed past him. She headed for the kitchen, turning on the lights over his kitchen table. "Okay if I fix myself a glass of milk?" asked Myrtle. She had just the faintest discomfort from heartburn.

"If you fix me one too," said Miles in a grudging tone. "And you might as well have a cookie, too. That will be the next thing you'll want, and it will help me fall back asleep again to have something in my stomach after you finally leave."

Myrtle ignored the *finally*. She poured them both a small glass of milk and took out a couple of cookies that were in his cookie jar on the counter. The chocolate chips were the huge kind.

"Sorry," she said. She looked down in what she hoped was appropriate remorse at her cookie as she broke it in half. She needed Miles on her side if she were going to bounce ideas off him. "Sorry about waking you up, I mean."

Miles raised his eyebrows and pushed his frameless glasses up his nose. "An apology? That's unusual, Myrtle."

"Well, I do feel bad. I simply assumed you were as shaken up as I was about the murder. I figured you were wide awake."

"Why would I be upset about Cosette?" asked Miles with a weary shrug. He nibbled delicately at his chocolate chip cookie. "No one seemed to like her much. She irritated people and flirted relentlessly with me, although I barely knew her. I do feel badly for Lucas, though. He certainly seemed very shaken up by the whole thing."

"Devastated," said Myrtle. "He seemed absolutely devastated. I can't imagine why, since she treated him horribly. I saw and heard her act very ugly to him." She took a thoughtful sip of her milk. "Have you ever heard of anyone with a specific complaint against Cosette?"

"Well…you."

"Yes, I know," said Myrtle. "I mean anyone *else*."

Miles pulled a small basket toward him and began folding cloth napkins on his kitchen table. "Let's see. Oh. How about Tobin Tinker? He lives right across from the Whitlow house, on our side of the street. He about talked my ear off one day about Cosette."

"Did he? About what?"

"It was a tale of trash," said Miles in a dramatic voice.

"Trash? You mean, like something trashy? Something dirty?"

"No. I mean *trash.* He was upset about his trashcan. Well, and upset about some other stuff, too, but I tuned him out at that point. Your Pasha was glaring at me from under Tobin's tree and I was afraid I might be attacked."

Pasha was the feral cat that Myrtle had befriended. She loved Myrtle. She cared little for Miles, however.

"Back to the trash, please."

"There's not a lot to tell." Miles sighed when he saw Myrtle wasn't going to give up.

"He said that it drove him crazy that Cosette used his trashcan."

Myrtle stared at Miles. "You mean the dumpster thing that we have to push out to the curb on trash day?"

"That's right. Apparently, Cosette frequently had extra trash—hosting all those parties, I suppose. She would put her excess bags of garbage in his receptacle."

Myrtle said, "Well, that's no motive for murder. That's just Tobin being a cranky neighbor."

Miles paused in his napkin folding. "He was very upset by it, Myrtle. Very, very upset."

"Why on earth for?"

"He seemed to think that Cosette was treating him like a peon because he's single and doesn't have as much trash.. He acted as though his feelings were hurt. He was also worried that the garbage man wouldn't pick up the overflow—

sometimes she put extra bags on the ground next to his can when it was really full."

Myrtle nodded. It was a legitimate concern. Since they were in such a small town, they each paid monthly for garbage collection out of their own pockets to a waste management contractor. And those folks could be picky about what they picked up, too.

"I can see the part about the extra trash on the ground being a problem. But who cares if she throws some extra garbage in his can if he has the space? He pays the same price for pickup whether the container is half-full or completely full. It's trash. Who cares?" Myrtle waved her hands in the air.

"Tobin does," said Miles solemnly.

"Miles, what do you think about neighbors who use other neighbors' trashcans?"

"I've never done such a thing," said Miles coldly.

"No, no, I'm not blaming you. I'm only asking. What do you think about a neighbor who has a lot of garbage bags, putting some extra bags in the neighbor's nearly empty container?" asked Myrtle.

"I think it's horrible," said Miles. "The thought of it sort of grosses me out. And it's my private property. I was completely shocked to discover that there were people who do this."

Myrtle nodded and drained the last of her milk. "Okay, so maybe trash can be construed as some sort of a weird motive. And there was definitely something going on with Sybil and Felix and Cosette. Lucas has to be a suspect because he's the husband. And Cosette's daughter, Joan, had an argument with her mom right before Cosette was killed. So here's what I'm thinking. I'll start nosing around some."

"*Start* nosing around?"

Myrtle ignored this bit. She'd gotten good at ignoring bits she didn't like. "Yes. I'll want to bring Joan a consolation casserole. And Lucas, too, of course. Food is always such a balm in times of great loss.

Miles's eyes were doubtful.

Myrtle stood up to go and then stopped short. "Miles!"

"What?"

"Do you remember what was on the Whitlows' front porch? When we were trying to leave the party, I mean?" asked Myrtle, feeling excitement wake her up again.

Miles frowned in concentration, pausing with his napkin folding. "A planter of impatiens?"

"No. A bag of trash! Blocking the door."

Miles nodded in remembrance. "That's so. But Lucas probably stuck it there—maybe he got interrupted in the middle of taking it out."

"Or maybe…Tobin was trying to make a point."

Chapter Five

Myrtle had a somewhat adversarial relationship with her collection of cookbooks. They took up gobs of space in her small kitchen and looked appropriately food-doused and brown with age…it *looked* like a serious collection of books for a serious cook. But Myrtle blamed these books for the intermittent culinary disasters that plagued her. The directions in the books were obviously unclear or even out-and-out wrong. With some trepidation, she pulled out the books and started leafing through them.

The recipes were fairly unimaginative. There were tons of chicken and broccolis, chicken and rice, meat loafs, and beef casseroles. Joan was sure to get at least ten casseroles and Lucas just as many. Maybe a soup? Soup could be lunch as well as supper, and Myrtle could make it in her slow cooker and not scorch it like she had the last time she'd tried making it.

She peered at the ingredients. Wonder of wonders, she seemed to have everything she needed for the potato soup. And, with an entire package of crumbled bacon, it *had* to taste good. Who didn't like bacon?

Myrtle was well into making the soup when her doorbell rang.

It was Elaine with Jack in tow. Myrtle pulled the door open. "Yay!" Jack said, beaming up at her.

"Yay!" she said back, leaning heavily on her cane so that she could give him a hug before he dashed inside.

"Are we interrupting anything?" asked Elaine. She had an armful of knitting paraphernalia with her and watched as Jack went straight to Myrtle's coat closet to pull out his basket of toys. "I thought we might knit together while Jack plays. After the day you had yesterday, I figured that a very calming activity was in order."

She turned and beamed at Myrtle. Elaine's face looked positively thrilled. "Oh my," said Myrtle.

"Red told me how excited you were to return to knitting!" said Elaine, beaming at her. "I'm so glad, Myrtle. I was hoping that you and I could spend more time together. We could keep an eye on Jack and knit and talk. It will be great!"

Myrtle sighed. Ordinarily, she'd interject that she hadn't the slightest interest in the hobby. She'd proclaim her anti-crafting stance. She'd fuss that Red was an insufferable busybody who needed to be stopped at all costs. The only problem was Elaine's complete and total delight. And the fact she'd mentioned that Myrtle could spend more time with Jack—one of Myrtle's main objectives in life at this point.

"Won't it?" she agreed weakly, looking at the basket with consternation. "Although, Elaine, you know I'm rusty. Quite rusty, since the last time I knitted was probably, oh, sixty years ago." And under duress. Her mother had insisted that she learn.

"That's not a problem. I'm really still learning, myself. I can help give you a refresher," said Elaine with a smile.

Myrtle felt an unfortunate flare-up of heartburn again.

"I brought over a few different kinds of supplies for you to try out. I know I sent Red over with a few, but I wanted to give you more options. Some knitting notions are a better fit than others," said Elaine.

Myrtle peered glumly into the basket, since she was clearly expected to show some interest in its contents. "These knitting needles are nice," she said, pulling them out. They were silver, sharp, and about four and a half inches long.

Elaine grinned at her. "I might have known you'd pick those wicked-looking needles. The nicest thing about those is that they're hollow, so they're lightweight and easy to use." Elaine bent to hand Jack another truck that had somehow gotten mixed up in the knitting supplies.

"Besides bringing the knitting stuff over, I wanted to let you know that Red was really pleased that you told him about Mary Marlson's memory issue. Sure enough, the clothes that she swore were stolen from her clothesline were safe and sound in her closet."

"I suppose she was all defensive about it and swore that fairies had put the clothes in there," said Myrtle.

Elaine snorted. "Fairies? I don't think so. But yes, she was defensive about it and Red said she didn't even apologize for wasting his time."

"She told me fairies had put her lost marble in her pocket," muttered Myrtle.

"What? Oh, the lost marble. Yes, Red said something about that to me. No, no mention of fairies this time…which was probably a good thing, considering her age and all."

"Yes. One serious mention of fairies could put you in the Greener Pastures Retirement Home at our age," said Myrtle.

Elaine laughed. "I suppose so. Well, do you want to knit in the living room, or in the kitchen?"

Fortunately, Myrtle had an excellent excuse not to knit. "I'm actually cooking some food for Lucas Whitlow and Joan. But feel free to knit while I cook. Do you want Jack to bring the toys into the kitchen to play so we can keep an eye on him?"

"Oh, okay. That's nice of you to make something for them. Keeping an eye on Jack might be a good idea. He's been really getting into stuff lately. Jack, why don't you bring your trucks in the kitchen?" asked Elaine.

So they settled into Myrtle's sunny kitchen. It was a cozy scene with Elaine knitting, Jack making truck noises to himself, and Myrtle busying herself over the large slow cooker. She tossed in a bag of shredded hash browns. They were frozen, but she double-checked the recipe and it definitely said frozen. Unfortunately, she didn't check the recipe before adding the entire envelope of ranch dressing mix instead of the one tablespoon the recipe called for. Although Myrtle did notice that it looked odd to have all the seasoning floating on top of the soup, so she stirred the mixture vigorously before putting the top on the slow cooker.

Unfortunately, that was all the cooking that was required. Myrtle sat down with Elaine at the kitchen table and reluctantly picked up the knitting needles that Elaine had given her, and the bright blue yarn. "Let's see," said Myrtle, frowning fiercely at the yarn. "I need to make the first row. Right."

"Start with a slip knot," said Elaine brightly. "Oh, I'm so excited about this."

Myrtle promptly dropped a needle on the floor and then dropped the yarn as she was hanging upside down to retrieve the needle. She started to mutter a dire imprecation under her breath, but remembered how excited Elaine was and managed to come back up with both needles, the yarn, and a smile. The smile might have resembled more of a snarl, but she was definitely trying.

Since Myrtle had many decades ago discarded how to make a slip knot from her brain, she stared blankly at the yarn until Elaine showed her how to do it. "Then you cast on your foundation row."

Myrtle gave her a despairing look. "Oh, Elaine. I just don't know about this."

"Myrtle, it's so easy! Sooo easy. Let me show you on yours," Elaine dropped her own knitting (which resembled a gangly scarf that was far, far too long), and worked with Myrtle's knitting for a couple of minutes. "See?"

Myrtle did see, but she'd rather not see. "You know, Elaine, I think it was the crazy day yesterday. I don't seem to have the ability to focus on anything."

Elaine smiled at her. "That's why knitting is so perfect. Once you get into the groove of it, it comes almost automatically. And it's wonderful for people who have nervous energy."

"I don't know that I'm *nervous*—just distracted. Elaine, you probably knew Cosette better than I did. What did you think of her?"

Elaine continued knitting, smiling over at Jack every once in a while as the little boy drove his truck across the kitchen floor. "I didn't know her all that well, actually. But I ran across her at the church and my service organization—places like that. She was hugely into volunteering you know. She was always in charge of something. Cosette could organize an event like nobody else."

"So she was bossy," said Myrtle, feeling like that summed it up the best.

Elaine laughed. "Well, she liked to do things her way. But her way was apparently the best way to do it, because all the events she'd organize—fundraisers, get-togethers, lectures, whatever—would go off without a hitch."

"What was her relationship with her husband like?" asked Myrtle, watching as Jack made the truck crash into a toy car.

"Lucas always seemed like he was a real pushover," said Elaine with a shrug, "although, he's a very sweet guy. A few weeks ago at the church, I was struggling to carry a basket of old baby toys to donate to the nursery and hold Jack's hand at the same time. Cosette swept right by as if she didn't even see me, but Lucas stopped to take basket and help me out."

"It doesn't sound like Lucas had a choice about being a pushover. It was either he had to go along with whatever

Cosette had planned, or get mowed over in the process," said Myrtle. "She probably married him because he wouldn't stand up to her."

"Probably. She wouldn't have appreciated any resistance. You know how I'm on different volunteer committees and things. Cosette tended to take over everything. Really. It's amazing to behold. Of course, her ideas always worked out, so no one dared say anything. But even if she weren't the committee chair, she'd usurp their position. She was really something. And I've heard her fussing at Lucas, too—complaining about his weight and how boring he was and how he wasn't ambitious enough. He would always look so sad and simply nod his head as if he were agreeing with her," said Elaine.

"I'm beginning to wonder how these committees are going to get along without her," said Myrtle.

"I suppose that the women who were *supposed* to be running the committees will have to step in," said Elaine, finishing a row of knitting. She looked up at Myrtle. "I know you're trying to gather information on Cosette. Planning on doing some investigating? Are you on assignment for Sloan?"

Myrtle knew there'd been something she'd forgotten to do this morning. "No, I keep forgetting to call him up. I walk toward the phone, and then I get distracted by something and end up doing something else. But I'm sure that Sloan will want me to write a story once he hears that I'm the one who found the body."

"Tell me what happened last night," said Elaine. "I got the bare bones of the story, but Red wasn't in the mood to elaborate."

"He was probably dead tired by the time he finally got back home," said Myrtle. "He seemed bent on interviewing everybody there, and that was a lot of people. So, when

Miles finally was ready to drag me out of the party, we went looking for Cosette to thank her. We couldn't find her—until we *did* find her."

Elaine gave a small shudder. "Red said she'd been struck with a croquet mallet. That's awful."

It was always nice when Elaine accidentally confirmed information via Red. "Is that what Red told you? It certainly looked that way to me, yes."

"Any ideas who might have done it?" asked Elaine. "Would there have been much opportunity to have killed the hostess of a big party? The whole thing sounds kind of unbelievable."

"Honestly, I think anyone could have done it. There were lots of people moving around at the drop-in—folks going for more food, going to the restroom, moving around to talk to other people. You know how parties are. No one would have noticed if someone had slipped outside," said Myrtle.

"But wouldn't people have noticed that *Cosette* had stepped outside? She was the hostess."

"Let's just say that they probably wouldn't have noticed her *absence*. If they did, they'd likely have chalked it up to the fact she needed to get more ice or something." Myrtle paused. "Can you think of anyone who might have wanted to kill Cosette? Any of those committee women, for instance? Seems like they'd have been plenty upset about Cosette poaching on their territory."

Elaine pursed her lips in thought. "Not really, Myrtle. Not *that* upset."

"Have you heard anything about Sybil being mad at Cosette?"

Elaine raised her eyebrows in surprise. "Sybil was mad at Cosette?"

"Never mind," said Myrtle with a sigh. "You're sadly out of touch with local gossip, Elaine."

"Jack keeps me so busy that I hardly know if I'm coming or going," said Elaine.

Myrtle drummed her fingers on the table. "How about Cosette's daughter? Aren't y'all friends?"

"Joan? Oh, sure, we're friends. Noah and Jack are the same age, so I do see more of Joan," said Elaine.

"What do you think Joan's relationship with her mother was like?" asked Myrtle. "It sounded like Cosette was fussing at her on the phone."

"That would be normal for them. Cosette was always fussing at Joan, just like she always fussed at Lucas. Poor Joan was apparently nothing like Cosette thought she should be. She doesn't dress very well, doesn't get flattering haircuts, isn't slim. Cosette always acted like Joan was a huge disappointment," said Elaine.

"Maybe that's why Cosette was pouring so much attention into Noah," mused Myrtle. "Although *clearly*," she said, beaming down at her grandson, "Jack is much more advanced in every way."

After Elaine left, Myrtle peered into the crockpot at the soup. It certainly *seemed* done. She picked up the recipe. Yes, it had sat in there for two hours on high, so it must be done. And it smelled delicious. All those seasonings…they seemed to open up her sinuses.

Myrtle poured the soup into two disposable storage containers. She paused, looking thoughtfully at the containers. Ordinarily, she'd put something like this into a throw-away containers so no one would have to worry about returning it to her in their time of grief. But, if she used one of her own good containers, she'd have an excellent excuse for a return visit to both Lucas and Joan. She carefully poured the soup into her nice blue and white containers and marked her name on them with masking tape.

She'd stuck her head into the pantry to find a sleeve of crackers to send along with the soup when her doorbell rang.

Miles stood on her doorstep. "You left your sweater at my house last night," he said, holding up the white cardigan.

Myrtle frowned at it. "I swear I'm turning into a comet…leaving bits and pieces behind me in my wake." She took the sweater and tossed it at the back of a chair, where it promptly slid behind the chair and out of sight.

Miles sniffed the air cautiously. "You've been cooking?" he asked with some trepidation.

"Yes. Sympathy food for Lucas and Joan."

Miles's face did indeed show sympathy. Myrtle strongly suspected that Miles believed her to be a bad cook.

"Don't look so grim—it's not for you," she said with a sigh. "But it would be lovely if you'd drive me over to make my deliveries."

"Surely you don't need a ride to Lucas's house," said Miles. "He's right down the street."

"Yes, I *could* walk it, Miles. I have excellent mobility, as you know."

"Right. The cane is just for show," said Miles, corners of his lips twitching.

"It lulls people into a false sense of security," said Myrtle. "But the point is, that I have a hard time holding a container with one hand. Since I'm using my cane with the other, of course. And Joan lives pretty far away…I couldn't walk to her house."

Miles was already taking the containers from her and pulling his keys from his pocket.

They were halfway down the street when Myrtle barked, "Stop!"

Miles slammed on the brakes. "What? What is it?"

"Lemonade stand at the two o'clock position," said Myrtle in a calm voice, gesturing to a card table with two young children looking hopefully in their direction.

Miles sighed.

"I make it a rule to always stop for a lemonade stand," said Myrtle stoutly.

"Next time, could you alert me in a way that won't scare me half to death?" asked Miles.

"Don't be so cranky," said Myrtle, fishing a dollar from her purse. "I'll get you one, too."

When they got to Lucas's house, Myrtle carefully got out of the car and started to retrieve her container. "I'll be back in a few minutes," she said to Miles, closing the passenger door.

But Miles wasn't going to be so easily dispatched. "Knowing what a few minute's means to you, I think I'd better go in with you. By the time you came back out, I might be fossilized. Here, give me the soup."

Myrtle reluctantly handed over the container. "As long as you make sure Lucas knows that *I* was the one who made the soup. Not you."

"I'll be *sure* not to claim the soup," said Miles with a small smile as he reached up to ring the bell.

Chapter Six

A very small, fluffy-looking old lady answered the door. She gave them a bright smile. "You're here to see Lucas I suppose, aren't you, dears? I'm afraid he's not well and isn't up to seeing anyone. Won't you come inside? I'm his sister, Hazel." She beamed at them and opened the door wide.

For once, Myrtle didn't object to the endearment. Although she was very sensitive to being called sweetheart, dear, or darling by younger people, being called dear by a peer (even one a good fifteen years younger), wasn't as objectionable.

Myrtle was always most unsettled by old ladies who did the old lady act better than she did. This particular old lady was an excellent example. She wore her white hair back in a bun, wore green cat eye spectacles attached to a chain, a cardigan, pearls, and a sweet smile. Myrtle decided that the only thing that could possibly maker her even more of the old lady stereotype would be if she offered them milk and cookies.

"Can I interest y'all in some milk and cookies?" asked Hazel, her blue eyes twinkling behind the cat eye glasses.

"I'd love some," said Miles.

"I wouldn't mind some myself," said Myrtle. "I'll help you with them while I put my soup away. It's baked potato soup. Hearty stuff."

"Sounds scrumptious," said the little old lady with a tinkling laugh.

Myrtle put her soup in the fridge and set the crackers on the kitchen table. While Hazel was busily getting out some homemade cookies from a jar, Myrtle glanced out the kitchen window. There appeared to be a perfect view of the backyard from the window. Lucas could have easily spotted Cosette from here, bolted outside, killed her, and run back in to continue in the kitchen as if nothing had happened.

As she left the kitchen to go back to the small living room, Hazel chatting all the way, she saw that Lucas's bedroom door was tightly shut. She felt a pang. The poor, stodgy old fellow. He'd really seemed to care about Cosette—for whatever reason. Maybe the soup would actually be good for him if he felt so terrible.

Myrtle tuned back in to Hazel's rambling monologue. "It's such a tragedy, isn't it?" Hazel tutted.

Myrtle assumed Hazel was talking about Cosette's death. She said cautiously, "Well, death usually is. Very sad."

Miles rolled his eyes at her. She must have gotten the topic wrong.

Hazel blinked at her, all wide-eyed. "Oh dear. I'm mumbling again. Unless, you're hard of hearing, which I certainly am. I have to wear a special device."

Miles quickly interjected before they were subjected to a bellowing Hazel, "Myrtle isn't hard of hearing. Only hard of *listening*."

Hazel resumed her twinkling. "I see. Myrtle, I was only saying that it was tragic that there's been a delay in having a funeral. The police decided on an autopsy. I do think that funerals are wonderful for closure. Perhaps Lucas will feel some closure once we're able to properly celebrate Cosette's life with a service."

Myrtle nodded although she didn't believe in closure. It all sounded like psychology hocus-pocus to her. Time worked best, in her experience. As for funerals, she'd personally haunt anyone who treated hers as a cause for celebration. The very idea!

A change of subject was clearly in order. "You must be a huge help for Lucas right now. Are y'all very close?"

Hazel said, "We are, although I don't get a chance to visit as much as I'd like. I live in Charlotte, so it's a bit of a drive to Bradley. But I was here only a few weeks ago for a long weekend visit. So sad. I had no idea that would be the last time I'd see Cosette. Such a pity! She was such a sweet, sweet girl."

Myrtle looked closer at Hazel. She'd have thought her a bit young for dementia to have set in. Or perhaps she really *didn't* get to visit as often as she'd like, and didn't have a full picture of how awful Cosette actually was.

"Yes," said Miles, glancing with concern at Myrtle as if he thought she might start debating Cosette's sweetness, "she certainly was, wasn't she? Well, we hope that Lucas will be all right. It must have been a nasty shock for him."

"It was. Honestly, I was so very worried about his heart after a shock like that." Hazel started a ten-minute bout of babbling about Lucas's sensitive nature and various health complaints that he'd suffered in the past. Myrtle and Miles shared alarmed stares. What if they never escaped from here?

They both tuned back in to Hazel when she said, "...and it didn't help that Joan is misbehaving. That's making Lucas just about as sad as Cosette's death."

"How is Joan misbehaving?" asked Myrtle.

"Oh, I know people respond differently to death. The grieving process takes many forms, doesn't it? I suppose I'm rather matter-of-fact about Cosette's death, myself, although I did get quite teary-eyed at the start," said Hazel.

Myrtle was hoping to deflect another dip into the psychology of grief. "Certainly understandable. But what about Joan?"

"She's acting relieved," said Hazel with a confusing knitting of her brow. "In fact, she *said* she was relieved. This was rather hurtful to Lucas, as you can imagine. His own daughter basically saying that she was glad that her mother was dead!"

Hazel looked as if she might tear up. Myrtle said, "Did they not have a good relationship, then?"

"Cosette always had a family get-together when I was in town, so we had one for my most recent visit. Noah was playing with Cosette and Joan looked rather surly, I'm afraid. She didn't say much. She was always such a hard person to get to know. A very quiet child, a remote teenager. Joan was given every advantage, every privilege and she seems to have squandered them. Or at least, has certainly not appreciated them," said Hazel, looking bewildered.

Miles said carefully, "Yes, I wondered about that. It seems like Cosette and Lucas must have sacrificed a lot over the years. Myrtle was telling me that Joan had a big debut and a big wedding."

Hazel sighed. "Yes, and they also provided Noah with every opportunity, too. Sacrifice is definitely the word. Lucas has told me," said Hazel in a gossipy whisper, "that he's in rather dire financial straits. They showered money on Noah—money they didn't have…which is why he's such an advanced little guy. What a wonderful child! I treasure the time I spend with him."

Myrtle was now truly worried that the conversation would veer off into 'extraordinary Noah' territory. She quickly said, "Joan wasn't interested in being a society woman, I take it?"

"She never appreciated the scrimping and saving her parents did to give her every advantage they could. Instead, she's almost thrown it back in their faces. It must really have hurt Lucas and Cosette, I'm sure. And—bless her heart—but she's nobody's pretty child. Maybe that's why she was so dreadfully awkward at parties. Still, Cosette and Lucas kept right on giving everything they could to Joan and Noah. Did you hear about the special tutors that child has?" asked Hazel, face brightening. "It's really extraordinary how they've found teachers to help encourage his gifts. He's already a wonder on the piano, and picks up languages in a second."

It seemed like there was nothing else of substance that they were going to get from Hazel today. Miles looked over at Myrtle and said, "So sorry to interrupt, Hazel, but I think it's time for us to head out. Myrtle and I have more soup to deliver."

Myrtle fumbled for her cane and was already out on the doorstep when she turned to thank Hazel for the milk and cookies. She raised her eyebrows when she saw Miles leaning over and whispering something in Hazel's ear. He seemed to be gesturing in the general vicinity of the kitchen. Myrtle refused to be paranoid, although she had the sneaking suspicion that Miles might be maligning her soup.

"Soup? That's awfully nice of you," said Joan, pushing her thick glasses up her nose and giving Myrtle and Miles a shy smile, stepping aside to let them into her home. "I'm sure the soup will really hit the spot. I was beginning to get tired of the chicken divan that the church ladies were bringing over. What a nice change. I'll pop this in the fridge and then we can have a little visit. Noah is napping, so it's the perfect time to talk. Have a seat."

Joan went off to the kitchen, humming as she went. Yes, people did react to grief in different ways as Hazel had mentioned, but it sure seemed that Cosette's death had put a spring in her daughter's step.

Myrtle and Miles glanced around the small den for a place to sit down. Most of the furniture was covered with toys of all types and descriptions. The furniture itself, Myrtle noticed, looked to be both new and expensive, especially for a single mom on a preschool teacher's budget. Had Cosette and Lucas pitched in for the furniture, too? It seemed like a given that the toys came from the doting grandparents.

"I thought we might want something to drink," said Joan, coming back from the kitchen holding a small tray with tall glasses full of cola.

She'd already poured it, so Myrtle felt she couldn't really turn it down. A visit to the powder room might be in order shortly, considering they'd had lemonade starting out on their visits, and then milk at Lucas's house. Miles and Myrtle took the glasses with a smile. Then Myrtle cleared her throat. "We're so sorry about your mother," she said, trying to summon the appropriate concern. She didn't want to overdo it, either, since Joan herself didn't appear very distraught. "I was trying to think of something I could do to help you out. Could I watch Noah for you? Give you a break one afternoon?"

Joan said, "That's really sweet of you, Miss Myrtle. People always offer help, but so rarely offer something specific. It would be wonderful if you could watch Noah for me during Mother's funeral. I believe it will be a couple of days from now. I'd hate to have to bring him to the funeral."

Myrtle gulped, but nodded. Now she'd really done it. She'd thought that her babysitting offer would be a good way to see more of Joan and get another shot at questioning her later. But she'd had every intention of being at that funeral and to see if anyone looked guilty, gossiped, or gave her any new leads. "Of course," she said weakly. "I'd be delighted to watch Noah."

Joan slapped her forehead. "Oh, wait a minute. I must be losing my mind. I forgot that Elaine already offered to keep Noah for me so that he and Jack can have a play date. But thanks for your offer."

Myrtle relaxed. "Well, is there another time I can help you out?"

Joan said, "If you don't mind, I did tell my dad that I'd help him go through Mother's things. I'd called him yesterday and he mentioned that the thought of going through her clothes was making him even sadder. If that's possible."

Myrtle said, "That sounds perfect. Give me a call and let me know when you want to bring him by. Maybe I can even have Jack over then to give them the chance for another play date. That way, I could help Elaine out at the same time."

Joan laughed, "They're really both at the age where they're doing parallel play instead of interacting with each other. You'll see Jack pushing his truck around and Noah pushing his, but the trucks will never intersect. But I think they enjoy being around each other, anyway."

"It's settled then," said Myrtle, beaming at her.

Miles said, "Joan, I'm glad you're helping poor Lucas out. We tried to visit with him before we came here, but he was too upset to come out."

"He's definitely taking it hard, but then Dad has always been crazy over Mother. I've never really been able to figure that out, since she was always fussing at him. Always telling him to tuck his shirt in more, or to stand up straight, or to lose weight." Joan looked ruefully down at her own pear-shaped figure. "I heard the same stuff. I do know one thing, though. He'd never have laid a finger on her, no matter what the police think. He worshipped the ground she walked on, no matter how she treated him."

Myrtle said, "Is there anything you can think of that could help the police find the murderer? Redirect them to another suspect? I have insider connections, you know."

"Red has been great, Miss Myrtle. But I have a feeling the state police think that Dad is behind the whole thing. There should be plenty of good suspects, though. Mother was hard to like. But yes, there was one thing that I need to tell the police about," said Joan.

Myrtle leaned forward in her chair.

"Since I've gotten divorced," said Joan, "I've needed help around the house and yard. The yard has been especially tough for me to stay on top of, so I made a call to a yardman that I found in the phone book to get an estimate for weekly yard work. As a matter of fact, he lives right across from Mother and Dad."

Miles frowned. "Tobin, is it?"

"That's right. Tobin Tinker. He came right on time and gave me a good estimate. But he was completely preoccupied with my mother and the problems he was having with her as a neighbor. He listed all kinds of stuff—she had too many parties and her guests blocked his driveway with their cars. That the parties were too loud and kept him up at night. And he said that she kept putting her excess trash in his garbage can…he was particularly upset about that."

Myrtle hoped that maybe she had some more information than they did. "Extra trash?"

"Well, you know how we're supposed to put *all* our trash in the roll-out cans? No bags on the ground? Mother had lots of extra trash sometimes because of her parties. She'd apparently stick the extra bags in Tobin's trashcan. He lives alone and I guess he doesn't have enough garbage to fill up his own can," said Joan. She rolled her eyes. "It was kind of ridiculous of Mother to do that, but I can see her doing it."

"But why was he telling you all of this?" asked Miles. "Sounds like he was just dumping on you."

"I suppose he thought I had Mother's ear and that she'd actually listen to me. He looked crushed when I told him that Mother had made a point of never listening to anything I said. Anyway, he made me so uncomfortable with this anger he was displaying that I decided not to call him back to do the yard work. I don't really want someone with a temper hanging out around Noah," said Joan.

Myrtle said, "Makes sense to me." She was still thinking back to the big bag of overflowing trash that had been on the Whitlows' front porch.

"Do you know any yardmen who could help me out?" asked Joan.

Myrtle laughed. "I like you too much to foist my Dusty on you. And Miles still manages to do his own yard somehow."

"Dusty isn't all that bad," said Miles. "At least he's not as bad as Puddin."

"Yes, Dusty's wife, Puddin, cleans my house for me. Although *cleaning* is an exaggeration. She never actually accomplishes more than pushing the dust from one side of a table to another. But Dusty does a fair job on the yard when he actually comes. It's hard to get him to come over, though. When you call him, he yowls that it's too wet to mow, even if it hasn't rained in months."

"Sounds like a problem I don't need," said Joan with a grimace. "I'll keep looking out for somebody."

Myrtle was trying to figure out how to get off the yardmen conversation and back to the murder when Joan suddenly looked penitent. "Oh, shoot. I completely forgot to make sure *you're* doing all right, Miss Myrtle. I hear that you were actually the person who discovered the body." She said it very matter-of-factly, looking steadily at Myrtle behind those thick lenses.

Myrtle's eyes widened over the use of the word *body* instead of *mother*. "Yes, I'm afraid I did. Along with Miles and your father, of course. It was quite a shock. But I'm so glad that you weren't the one to discover her, Joan. We saw you arrive there, but knew you'd left."

Joan flushed. "I didn't behave very well that night. Mother and I have never been close. She never really understood me. She thought I should have been the Magnolia

Queen, snagged the perfect, wealthy husband, and started being some kind of society matron. Instead, I married a plumber for love. The love didn't last for very long." She shrugged. "I was a huge disappointment to her."

Myrtle wanted to pooh-pooh that statement, but she knew it wouldn't ring true. "But you did come to your mother's party when she asked you to. And I know she was proud as punch of Noah."

"I didn't want to go, though. I had a million things to do at home, instead. I had to cut out construction paper shapes for my preschool kids the next day, do laundry, clean the kitchen—and run errands, too. I was out of bread, and Noah and I always pack sandwiches for lunch. But this time Mother really pushed me to come. I went, but I decided to take advantage of the fact that I had someone to watch Noah for me and I ran off to at least get the stuff I needed from the store," said Joan.

"And you never made it back to the drop-in?" asked Myrtle.

"Well, I had refrigerated items, so I ran back home to put those things away. While I was there, I thought I could get started cutting out the shapes for preschool and doing the housework. I know it was bad of me, but Mother made me so angry. The next thing I knew, someone from the police was at my door, telling me about Mother's death," Joan shrugged, looking away.

Miles gave Myrtle a quick glance that told her he was thinking the same thing she was—Joan was keeping a secret.

Chapter Seven

The next morning, Myrtle picked up the phone and called Sloan Jones, her editor at the *Bradley Bugle*. It was time to find out more about this reporter he'd been talking about at the drop-in.

"*Bugle*," drawled Sloan, sounding as if he might be munching on his lunch.

She said, "Sloan, it's Myrtle."

Sloan's voice became more alert, as it always did whenever Myrtle addressed him. Myrtle had been his English teacher many years ago and he'd never managed to put the experience behind him. He'd had a terrible time remembering to turn in his homework that year, and never could recite that soliloquy from *Hamlet* to her satisfaction. He'd passed the class by the skin of his teeth and she'd been relieved to be done with him. She'd been pretty appalled when he'd ended up as editor and publisher of the town's newspaper, especially considering his background in English. Red had persuaded Sloan to give Myrtle a weekly helpful hints column for the paper—mostly to keep Myrtle out of trouble. Sloan had let Myrtle write investigative stories for the *Bugle* a few times, too.

"Miss Myrtle," he said, "how are you doing? I was just thinking that I needed to get in touch with you about your column this week. How's it coming along? You know that there'll practically be a riot in the streets if we miss including your helpful hints this week."

"I'm sure they'll live," said Myrtle dryly. "Actually, I was thinking about doing a bigger story this time. The Whitlow murder. I'm assuming you're already working on a story about it, but I'd like to take it over. I'm going to find out who's behind Cosette Whitlow's murder."

Sloan sounded like he might be experiencing some stomach upset. "The Whitlow murder? Miss Myrtle, you must have better things to do than to get involved with that story."

"Better things to do? What? Play bingo at the community center? Watch the last episode of my soap another time? What *better things to do* could I possibly have?" asked Myrtle.

"Well, you know, your helpful hints column is getting so popular that I thought we might want to run it more than once a week. People are really eating that stuff up."

Myrtle's voice became sharper. "Sloan, are you trying to get me out of the newsroom? Because I'd much rather be poking my nose into the Whitlow murder than telling people how to get tomato sauce stains out of their clothes."

Sloan meekly said, "You see, Miss Myrtle, I have this new intern. She's from Atlanta and is trying to get bylines and clips so that she'll have something for her portfolio when she interviews with the Atlanta paper."

Myrtle frowned. "So she's getting the top stories: and what are you getting?"

She could picture Sloan blushing on the other end of the wire—that red, splotchy flush that went all the way up to the top of his ever-expanding forehead. "Miss Myrtle, it's not like that. Kim is right out of college…she's just a kid. You see—I don't have to pay her anything since she's an intern. Plus, she's really sharp."

"You barely pay *me* anything. And I'm really sharp, too. Besides, I'm the one who discovered Cosette Whitlow's body. And my son is the town's police chief. It sounds like I'm the one who should be writing the story—not some kid from Atlanta who doesn't even know these people."

Sloan sounded apologetic. "I'd undo it if I could, Miss Myrtle, but she's already reporting the story. Seems kind of harsh just to take her right off it, especially since we had a deal. I didn't know you were the one who discovered the body. I'll get Kim to interview you straightaway."

"Don't bother. No comment. I'll write my own story and then you can choose the story you'd rather run at the end of the case."

"I'm sorry, Miss Myrtle," said Sloan regretfully. He was sure he'd be paying for this at some point in the future.

"I know you are. See you soon, Sloan."

"Wait! Miss Myrtle, what about the helpful hints column? Is it ready?" pleaded Sloan.

She certainly didn't have any time to research a bunch of helpful hints for the old biddies in the town. She'd have to make some up. "Fine. I'll email it to you tonight," said Myrtle. She could put something together in five minutes if she didn't have to look it up.

She hung up, and then pulled her phone book out of her desk. If Tobin Tinker had some grievances against Cosette, she'd like to hear them. It was going to be tricky having a rival yardman come to her house, though. Dusty wouldn't like it. She couldn't afford to lose Dusty, despite his deplorable work ethic. He was cheap, did a decent job, and was the only yardman in town who'd trim weeds around her gnome collection.

But Myrtle saw in the phone book that Tobin also apparently offered tree removal services. She peered out the back window. There was a sickly-looking pine tree down by the lake that had been ailing for some time. Ordinarily, she'd simply let nature take its course, especially since the tree was in no danger of falling on her house or anyone else's. But she could always call Tobin to get an estimate for removal. She picked up the phone again.

Tobin answered promptly and listened as she outlined the tree problem. "I'd be happy to come take a look at it. I'm pretty booked-up this week, though, unless you're free for me to run by right now. Since you're right down the street, I could take a look at the tree real quick before I head out to the next job."

"That would be great. I just want to get an idea how much it would cost to take it down."

When they hung up, Myrtle smiled. Now to get him to rant a little about Cosette. It should be easy enough to broach the subject since they were both neighbors of hers.

Tobin was there in a couple of minutes and went straight to the backyard. He was a solid, big man, well over six feet tall. He had a broad face and was brown from the sun. He peered down the hill to the spot Myrtle was pointing at. "That scraggly pine tree down there near the lake?" he asked. "Ordinarily, it'd be between six hundred and fourteen-hundred to bring her down. But that pine tree is so pitiful that I'll take it down for three-hundred for you. When do you want me to take care of it?"

He'd given her such a low price that he clearly expected her to jump on it. Three hundred was really cheap, but it was very expensive if you didn't really need to have the work done. "Let me see. I'll have to save up for a while to be able to pay you. Retired schoolteachers don't make a whole lot, unfortunately."

Tobin looked at the tree again. "That should be fine, since that tree isn't going to fall on your house or your neighbors'. Give me a call when you're ready to cut it down."

"I will, and thanks. By the way, what do you make of Cosette Whitlow's murder? You're right across the street from her, aren't you? So shocking!" said Myrtle.

Tobin flushed and looked away. "I'll admit I wasn't much of a fan of hers. Although I'm sorry she's dead, of course." His voice wasn't very convincing.

Myrtle had hoped he wouldn't worry about speaking ill of the dead. She took on a more gossipy tone. "Did you know that I'm actually the one who found the body? Such an awful thing. And I did feel so sorry for Lucas. He seemed crushed."

Tobin nodded and relaxed. "I always did feel bad for poor Lucas, living with that woman. I've had plenty of run-ins with Cosette, but Lucas has always been a great guy and a good neighbor."

"What kind of run-ins did you have with her?" asked Myrtle. She gave an exaggerated sigh. "Here at the other end of the street, I can never keep up with all the news."

Tobin looked ill at ease again. "Well, I don't know as I should say anything, Miss Myrtle. Seeing as how she's dead and everything."

Myrtle acted as if she hadn't heard that mild reproof. "Cosette Whitlow irritated me too, you know."

"Is that so, Miss Myrtle?"

"First of all…well, also second and third and one-hundredth of all…she was annoying," said Myrtle simply.

Tobin started applauding and Myrtle gave a bob of her head in acknowledgment.

"Well put, Miss Myrtle," said Tobin with a barking laugh. "That's exactly what she was. Annoying. We'll call a spade a spade."

"The way she went on and on about her daughter and her grandson…" Myrtle snorted. "The daughter was the perfect debutante and the grandson will surpass Einstein as the greatest modern-day thinker."

There was that barking laugh of Tobin's again. "I'll have to take your word on that, since I never had a civilized conversation with her."

Myrtle raised her eyebrows. "Never? What kinds of conversations did you have with Cosette?"

"Oh, the neighborly kind. You know."

Myrtle did know. And she knew that Tobin didn't mean *friendly neighbor kind*, he meant the *warring neighbor kind.* "She was getting on your last nerve, wasn't she?"

For a startled moment, Myrtle worried that the big man was going to start crying, right there in her yard. "It was a nightmare, that's what it was, Miss Myrtle. That yippy dog of hers barked all hours of the day and night. I left a polite note on her door explaining that Scamp was clearly upset and needed to spend more time inside."

"It didn't help?" asked Myrtle sympathetically.

"After I left the note, that Scamp was outside even more. Barking his furry head off, he was. He barked whenever the wind blew," said Tobin sorrowfully. "Thank goodness he ended up passing away from old age. I was about to call Red up and get the police involved."

"Barking would have driven me batty," said Myrtle. "Of course, I live next to the infamous Erma Sherman, so I don't exactly have a good neighbor, myself." She was prepared to give Tobin the lowdown on Erma's inadequacies as a neighbor, but he was still completely wrapped up in Cosette.

"Another thing that drove me up the wall—Cosette used my trash can. She always had extra trash—having all those parties, you know. She knew I'm a single man," Myrtle swore she saw Tobin's lip tremble at this last bit, "and that I don't have a lot of trash to put out, living alone and all. So Cosette put her extra bags of garbage in my container. It stuck out the top. Once she even put a bag beside my trashcan since she had so many piled next to her own. I was always worried the garbage man wasn't going to pick them up."

"A couple of times the garbage man left the extra bags, so I took them to the dump myself. I couldn't stand the sight of the garbage piled up in front of my house," said Tobin.

"You know," said Myrtle slowly, "there was a bag of trash at the drop-in. It was absolutely overflowing. I thought the placement of it was rather odd—blocking their front door."

Tobin flushed, and quickly made a slight change of topic. "And it wasn't only the dog and the trash can either, although those would be bad enough. Like I was saying, she had people over all the time—brunches and bridge and cookouts and stuff. Her guests parked on both sides of the street and sometimes even blocked my driveway so I couldn't pull my truck out. Then her parties always ended up in her backyard and I could hear the folks laughing and cutting up until the middle of the night. I'm a hard-working fellow, Miss Myrtle, and I need my sleep." Tobin's face looked hurt. "All I want to do after a hard day of work is to watch some TV or maybe look at my baseball card collection. I'm as quiet as can be—why couldn't Cosette Whitlow be?"

"Very, very annoying. Yes. Neighbors can be a trial, can't they? When I was telling Erma what a nuisance her crabgrass was...."

"And that's another thing. When her guests parked on my side of the street, their tires trenched my yard. She'd seen me out there with a shovel before, trying to fix it and smooth it over a little and she laughed and kept on driving. Didn't even roll down her window to ask if she could send her husband over to help."

Myrtle was now very worried that Tobin was going to cry. She had never been very good with women who cried, and she was sure that she wasn't going to handle having this big man sobbing in her backyard.

"Poor Lucas," said Myrtle, shaking her head. "Imagine living with someone like her. And loving her!"

"She yelled at the poor guy when she was with him. And she didn't spend *that* much time with him."

"Why do you say that?"

"Because she didn't. And I spotted her once with another man." He sighed. "There now, I've said too much. One of my resolutions this year was to stop making idle gossip, and here I am doing it."

"Aren't resolutions made to be broken?" asked Myrtle lightly, wishing that Tobin's conscience hadn't taken over at such a pivotal moment. "I have a tradition of making a resolution to walk every day. After sixty years of the same resolution, you'd think I'd keep it better."

But Tobin was steadfast. He didn't even give a bit of information when Myrtle asked him if he'd seen anything unusual at the Whitlow house the night Cosette died—he stared at her sideways, then gave her a written estimate and headed off to his next job.

Myrtle reluctantly decided to watch her newest episode of *Tomorrow's Promise*. It wasn't often that real life was more dramatic than her soap opera.

Before she could even go inside, though, she saw a rodent-like face peering over the fence at her. She jumped. "Erma!" she said crossly. "What on earth are you doing up there? You scared me half to death. And how *did* you get up there? That fence should be tall enough so that no one can peep over it." The fence was fairly new and she adored the privacy that it ordinarily afforded her.

Erma cackled at her. "I've got a stepstool here because I've been replacing light bulbs on my back porch. I heard voices, including a gruff, deep one, so I investigated. You've got a good neighbor in me, Myrtle. I'll make sure my elderly friend isn't in any danger. And you do get in danger sometimes, don't you? Red likes me to keep an eye open."

Myrtle rather felt as if she were in danger right now. And hearing that Red was employing Erma as some sort of spy made her even more irritated with him than she usually was. *If that were possible.* "Which reminds me. I need to give my gnomes an airing out."

Whenever Myrtle was unhappy with Red, which could be frequently, she laboriously pulled out her large collection of yard gnomes from the shed and put them throughout her yard. Red despised them and, since he lived diagonally across the street from her, got prime view of her civil disobedience.

Erma's face fell. "I was just thinking how lush your grass was finally looking since you haven't had the gnomes in the yard for a while."

"Except for the crabgrass, which is steadily encroaching from your yard," said Myrtle pointedly. "What did you want to talk with me about? I was heading in to watch my soap."

Erma knit her brow. "I heard you were the one who discovered Cosette's body at her party. It amazes me how you're always in the right place at the right time. Are you sure you're not manufacturing victims to give yourself something to do?"

"I fail to see how my distressing habit of discovering murder victims could be considered being at the right place and right time for anything," said Myrtle coldly. "It's nothing to laugh about anyway, with Lucas and Joan so upset."

"Joan is upset?" Erma snorted. "By the way, are you covering this for the *Bugle*? I know you've done crime stories for them in the past."

The faux-innocent look on her face told Myrtle that Erma knew about the new reporter. Myrtle wasn't going to give her the satisfaction of feeling like she knew more about the situation than Myrtle did. Although Erma likely did.

"Well, there's a cub reporter working on the story. I don't know if we can even call her a reporter since she's not being paid. She's an intern, I suppose. I'll write my in-depth coverage— my exposé—and she'll write up the basic news article with the who-what-when-where-why-how," said Myrtle. "Sloan naturally trusts me with the bigger, investigative stories. The intern can cover the factual account."

"You're being very generous about it," said Erma with her sneering smile. "I've heard that she's quite the hot-shot. Very young, smart, pretty, and active. A rising star."

The only part of those adjectives that stung was the *active*. Myrtle was extraordinarily active, but always had to have the addendum "for her age" attached to the word. "Sloan has had new, hot-shot reporters before," she reminded Erma. "They didn't go well."

"Sloan has her all over town looking for stories. I've seen her snapping photos all over town. He told me that she has a nose for news."

Myrtle said, "She'll have to in this town. Usually, news in Bradley consists of Georgia Summers finally taking down her Christmas decorations in July or that Ralph Morris plans on planting beans instead of tomatoes in his garden this year."

Erma apparently wasn't getting the kind of reaction she was hoping for. She returned to the murder. "Since you discovered the body and are doing the story and everything, I've got a tidbit to help you out."

"What's that?" asked Myrtle. Although she couldn't stand Erma and avoided her at every possible opportunity, she knew the woman did pick up a lot of gossip. It must have something to do with the large ears situated near the top of her head.

"A couple of weeks ago, I'd run by Cosette's house to pick up something for our garden club meeting."

Myrtle darkly considered Erma's crabgrass situation. Perhaps she should dig up a sample and show it to Erma's garden club.

Erma blithely ignored Myrtle's thunderous expression. "While I was in Cosette's house, there was this wild knocking on the door. Cosette yanked it open, and there was Sybil. An absolutely furious Sybil. She started shrieking at Cosette and calling her very rude names. But she stopped short as soon as she caught sight of me. She shot Cosette a death glare, gave me a not-very-nice look, and stormed off."

Myrtle said, "You have no idea why she was upset?"

"Not a bit, since all she was doing was name-calling. But Cosette seemed to know. Her face was real pinched and she slammed the door behind Sybil. I got out of there fast, let me tell you."

Suddenly, Erma blanched even paler than she usually was and her lips drew back in a snarl. Startled, Myrtle looked behind her and saw Pasha, her feral cat, standing close beside her and glaring menacingly at Erma. The cat was completely wild and hated everyone it laid eyes on except for Myrtle, alternately lunging at them and giving them death glares.

It adored Myrtle, however, which Myrtle had long ago convinced herself had nothing to do with the cans of cat food she lavished on the creature. Pasha would come in Myrtle's house and visit as long as Myrtle left a window cracked for her to escape when she wanted to. Everyone told Myrtle that Pasha, as a feral animal, would never behave as a real pet, couldn't be tamed, and wouldn't be good company for her in any way—that she should leave it to its own devices outside and not encourage it. Myrtle decided they didn't know what they were talking about, since Pasha was always a perfect love with her.

Erma, on the other hand, was no favorite of Pasha's. Erma also had a vicious allergy to all cats, particularly Pasha. This made Myrtle love Pasha even more.

Without saying goodbye, Erma stumbled off the stepladder and hightailed it through her back door.

"Kitty, kitty," called Myrtle tenderly, and Pasha bounded after her into the house. This time Myrtle decided a special treat was in order, and she bypassed the bag of dry kibbles for a can of premium albacore tuna.

Chapter Eight

The next morning, Myrtle sat at her breakfast table with a bowl of bran cereal, coffee, and a small notepad. She'd learned in the past that she needed to think about her investigating in an organized way. Thinking about the case, she figured that she needed to speak with Lucas pretty soon. He was, after all, the prime suspect. Perhaps fluffy Aunt Hazel would need to return to Charlotte at some point and Myrtle would get more of an opportunity to talk to him.

Today was the day that Joan was dropping Noah off so that she could help her father go through her mother's things. Myrtle realized she'd forgotten to call Elaine and ask if she'd like to drop Jack off at the same time so the two boys could have a play date. She squinted at her rooster wall clock. Eight o'clock. Elaine was surely up by now. Myrtle picked up her phone.

Elaine *was* up. In fact, she might have been up for the last few hours since she was already sounding tired. "Myrtle? What's up?"

Myrtle heard what sounded like loud singing in the background. "Is that Jack?"

"Oh, he learned *London Bridge* at preschool yesterday and now he's singing it over and over," said Elaine with a slightly hysterical laugh.

"That's nice," said Myrtle, not entirely sure that it was.

"Is it?" asked Elaine, not sure herself. "No, Jack. Eat your cereal—don't play with it."

Jack, ordinarily an exemplary toddler, sounded like he might be having an unusual day. Myrtle reassessed the situation. Did she really want *two* small boys in her small home this afternoon? But, as she remembered from many decades ago after her husband had passed away and she was rearing Red alone, it was easier in many ways to watch two children than one. They entertained each other. "Elaine, I'm watching Noah for Joan today. I thought you might want to bring Jack by and have some time for yourself." There. It was done and there was no going back now.

There was a pause on the other end of the line and Myrtle heard Jack saying, "Ka-boom! Ka-boom!" in the background. It was accompanied by the sound of some sort of object hitting Elaine's kitchen floor.

Then Elaine said, "Are you sure? Jack seems to have an excessive amount of energy today. Are you sure you want to watch *two* preschool-age boys?"

The doubt and concern in Elaine's voice made Myrtle even more convinced that not only *could* she do it, but that it was what she wanted most in the world at that moment. "Elaine, I'm positive. Jack is always as good as gold whenever he's with his Nana. And Noah, from everything I've heard, is a prodigy of some sort. Prodigies should be a breeze to watch."

There was a whooping on the other end of the line as Jack cheered over some unknown, unseen outcome in Elaine's kitchen. Elaine gave a deep sigh.

Myrtle said, "Look, you clearly need a break today. Think what you could do. You could run a Jack-free errand. You could tidy up Jack's room without him pulling out toys just as fast as you put them away. You could *knit*. You could…."

"Take a nap?" asked Elaine wryly.

"Naps are good, too. So may I borrow Jack for a while? It will actually help me out. Noah might get bored with only me to entertain him. And we know what happens when little boys get bored," said Myrtle.

There was a crashing sound in the background and Elaine said tersely, "I've got to go, Myrtle. Thanks for the offer. I'll drop him over soon. Call me if you have any trouble with him today and need to be rescued."

"Eleven-thirty, Elaine. Thanks." Myrtle put down the phone. She knew one thing—she sure wasn't going to be calling Elaine if she ended up in over her head. Not with all that doubt and concern in Elaine's voice, she wouldn't. Besides, these were small boys, and Myrtle had a lifetime of experience and wisdom to draw from. Everything would be fine.

Everything was not fine. It may have started out all right. Jack settled in nicely when Elaine brought him by. Then Joan showed up about twenty minutes later. She'd said chirpily, "You're so sweet to do this, Miss Myrtle. Dad is in such a state, and I know that clearing away some of Mother's things will do him a world of good. Noah has been very happy today, so I hope he won't be a handful." She gave Myrtle her cell phone number in case of any problems and she headed for the door.

Myrtle pressed her lips together. She'd hoped to have had a chance to talk to Joan before she'd run off. She'd have to try to talk to her when she came for pick-up.

Noah watched with interest as his mother stooped to wave goodbye. He *did* seem to be in excellent spirits. Myrtle beamed at him. "Hi Noah! Are you ready to have some fun? Jack is so excited about playing with you."

Noah looked at Myrtle, looked on as Jack played with a truck that Myrtle was to learn later would be a bone of contention between the two boys, and started a howling wail that made both Jack and Myrtle gape at him.

"I know what let's do!" said Myrtle, determined not to adopt an air of desperation this early in the process, "Let's have some milk and cookies!"

She knew the gambit would work, at least for a little while. Although she hated the way she felt like Hazel Whitlow while doing it.

The snack did work, but didn't last nearly long enough. Next, she pulled out some printer paper and old crayons and let them color. She'd forgotten, though, that this age group's idea of coloring was to scribble on a piece of paper for a couple of minutes before being ready to move on to something else.

They did play for a few minutes together—a few minutes of creative play with a blessed lack of conflict. That period was short-lived, however, when Noah decided to enact a hijacking and claim Jack's truck. Although Joan had sent Noah with a basket full of what were allegedly his favorite toys, he wanted nothing to do with any of them—he was quite vehement about that.

Wasn't Noah supposed to be a boy genius? Isn't that what Cosette had been so determined to impart to everyone whenever she came across them? "Want to show me what you know about French, Noah?" she asked brightly. Noah only cried harder.

Myrtle checked the clock. An hour-and-a-half to go. "How about some more cookies?" she asked, already pulling out the cookie jar again. She needed to buy some time until she could figure out what to do.

Miles. She could call Miles and get him to come over and help her out. She picked up the phone, but then hesitated. He'd never come over if he thought he was going to help her babysit. She thought it over and picked up the phone again.

"Miles. Hey. Do you think you could come by? Now. That's right. I just wanted to tell you what I found out from Erma. No, I'd rather talk about it in person. I'll tell you why when you get here." She hung up, hoping that she'd sounded mysterious enough to lure him over.

A few minutes later, the doorbell rang and Myrtle smiled. Miles stood on her doorstep, squinting quizzically. "So what's going on? You're not thinking your phones are bugged are you? Because that's kind of paranoid, if you are."

Myrtle said archly, "I'm thinking that I'm about eighty years older than my guests. And feeling it. I could use a hand."

She stepped to the side to reveal the two little boys sitting at her kitchen table.

"Oh no," said Miles. "Babysitting wasn't on my agenda today."

"Can't you add it on there? And I can fill you in on what I'm thinking about the case so far."

The boys picked that moment to finish eating and immediately proceeded to start chasing each other like wild things around Myrtle's small living room.

Miles wore an assessing look. "Sugar? You gave them sugar, Myrtle?"

"Feeding them seemed like the best way to keep them occupied at the time," said Myrtle with a shrug.

"Feeding them baby carrots with ranch dressing, maybe. Not sugar." With a put-upon expression, he walked to Myrtle's television set and punched the power button. He flipped the channels on the remote until he got to public broadcasting, which was miraculously playing a cartoon of some sort. Both boys ran over to plop on the floor in front of the set.

"*Voila*," he said, raising his eyebrows. "Magic."

Myrtle frowned. "Isn't that cheating? Shouldn't I be developing their minds and bodies and engaging them in creative pursuits?"

"At your age? No way. You're doing enough simply by making sure they're not destroying your stuff or setting the place on fire. And once they get tired of the television, which will be a while, then we'll crank *that* up," he said nodding his head at Myrtle's computer.

"Well, they're certainly mesmerized, I'll grant you that," said Myrtle grudgingly. The boys were practically frozen as they stared unblinkingly at the jolly animated dinosaur on the screen. "Thank goodness you're here."

He followed her to the kitchen and sat where he still had a view of the boys. "It's not often I hear those words from you, Myrtle."

Myrtle ignored that, bustling to the cabinet and fridge. "Here's your sweet tea. Now let's go over the facts of this case before utter chaos descends again."

She plopped down across from Miles and said, "Okay. So, Erma was pointing her stubby finger at Sybil, saying she witnessed her shrieking at Cosette and calling her all sorts of names."

"You've been talking with *Erma*?"

"Purely by accident," said Myrtle with a sniff.

"Hmm. Well, Erma's information does seem to jibe with what I've noticed about Sybil."

Myrtle blinked at him. "You've noticed something about Sybil? Why on earth haven't you told me that? Especially since we saw that little scene with Sybil at Cosette's party."

"Well, it's not like it's a lot of information. It's just that Sybil indicated that she wasn't exactly Cosette's number one fan."

Myrtle blinked at him in surprise. "Well, aren't you all full of local gossip? How unlike you, Miles!"

"I was paying attention at book club, that's all. Sybil Nelson was talking about Cosette. She was quite vicious," said Miles, thoughtfully.

"Interesting," said Myrtle. She plopped down in a kitchen chair to digest this news. "I have no idea why Sybil would be angry at Cosette. Wait, give me a clue."

Miles hesitated. "Boyfriend."

"That's my clue? Boyfriend? You could do better than that, Miles. Okay, clearly, her boyfriend, Felix, is having an affair with Cosette. So Sybil actually *said* that those two were seeing each other? At book club? How remarkable of her!"

"No, she didn't say anything about an affair. She said that Cosette was an insufferable braggart," said Miles.

This startled Myrtle even more than learning of the affair. "*Sybil*? Sybil used a phrase like 'insufferable braggart?' Somehow, I can't picture those words drawling out of her. I may have underestimated Sybil. All that loud laughter, hoop earrings, and costume-y peasant dresses misled me."

Miles said, "No, that was my summary of her actual words. She said something more along the lines that Cosette should learn to shut up and she thought she knew how to shut her up."

"Ahh. That sounds more like our Sybil. After all, she's the one who keeps forcing us to read all those incredibly imbecilic novels in book club."

Miles nodded. "She's the one."

"So she was upset at Cosette's bragging, too. No surprise there. How did you find out about the affair, then?" asked Myrtle.

"I must have looked surprised at how vicious Sybil was. She's usually kind of insipid, you know? But this was a really fierce attack on Cosette. I was getting some more iced tea and Erma came up to me and explained that Sybil's boyfriend was having an affair with Cosette," said Miles.

"Oh, now I understand why I didn't hear anything about all of this. I was starting to wonder if I'd spent the entire book club in the bathroom or something. If you were hanging around Erma, then I was obviously on the other side of the room, steering clear."

Miles said, "That's right. Remember? Erma was determined to drag you into conversation and you kept dashing off to get more food or to talk to someone else."

"But we have to remember that Erma is usually not the most reliable source of information. She tends to think that *everyone* is having an affair with everyone else. I'm not sure how much stock we can put into what she says. She might have made up this affair—it could be pure conjecture to explain the shouting Erma witnessed at Cosette's house. If that's the case, then what else do you think Sybil has against Cosette?" asked Myrtle. She absently rattled the ice cubes in her now-empty glass of tea.

"I've no idea," said Miles simply.

"You must have *some* thoughts on it," said Myrtle sharply.

"None at all."

"Use some creativity," said Myrtle.

"I wasn't blessed with an abundance of creativity," said Miles with a shrug. He hesitated. "Well, judging from what she said at book club, maybe…maybe she simply found Cosette…annoying." He gazed at Myrtle with a satisfied expression as if delivering a particularly deep analysis.

Myrtle sighed. "That's what *I* told you about Cosette. That would be *my* motive for killing her."

"If it's a good enough motive for you, it should be good enough for Sybil," said Miles. "Although I still think that Sybil doesn't seem very likely as a suspect to me."

"I think that Erma must be right. There must have been something going on between Felix and Cosette," said Myrtle.

"Or maybe Sybil simply suspects that there is. There sure was a lot of tension in that kitchen while we were in there."

"Don't remind me," said Miles, looking pained. "I don't know when I've ever felt so uncomfortable."

Myrtle continued, "As far as Sybil goes, I wish I could figure out a way for me to interview her without being completely obvious about it."

"There's always book club," said Miles.

Myrtle frowned. "Didn't we just have book club? Yes, I believe I suffered through it very recently. And we ended up with that ridiculous book to read."

"I only mean that you could invent a book club-related reason," said Miles.

"Such as?"

"I'm not sure. Tell her it's your turn to pick the book and you want her opinion on which of three novels you should choose."

"Isn't that a pretty weak excuse for a visit?" asked Myrtle.

Miles wasn't apparently in any mood to be delicate. "Myrtle, you're old. With age comes certain privileges."

"Not enough of them," grumbled Myrtle.

"I think you can get away with just about anything. So what if the excuse is a bit weak? You'll simply look like you have too much time on your hands and put too much stock in small things. She's still fairly new in town and doesn't even know you all that well, so she won't be suspicious over having you asking her opinion. Sybil won't know you're one of those ferociously clever old ladies," said Miles.

Myrtle rather liked the *ferociously clever*.

"Besides, it seems to me that you don't have to make up anything at all. You're a writer for the *Bradley Bugle*. Tell Sybil you're working on a story for the paper. That would even be the truth, wouldn't it?"

"Oh sure, Miles. That's certain to make Sybil open up about her boyfriend's affair—talking to a member of the press. No, she seems like the type to clam up if she's talking to a reporter, even a reporter like me. Remember, she's a *suspect* in a murder investigation. And her boyfriend was having an affair with the victim, as far as we can tell. None of that seems like stuff she'd want to have blabbed around town in the local paper."

"I guess you should stick with the book club excuse, then."

"Maybe Felix will be over there and I can interview him, too," said Myrtle thoughtfully.

"That'll never work out. She's not going to tell you anything while he's around. Maybe you can catch him at work and somehow broach the subject."

"What does Felix do again?" asked Myrtle.

Miles seemed to be repressing a sneeze. Or a laugh. "He sells life insurance."

"That might work." Miles's laughter was obvious now. "Miles, the way people are living, I could live another twenty years or more, easily."

Miles apparently decided to avoid that subject. "Who are you favoring as a suspect, Myrtle?" asked Miles as he leaned forward in his chair to make sure that the boys were still engulfed in the cartoon. They were.

"Tobin Tinker," said Myrtle decidedly.

"What? Tobin?"

"I talked to Tobin at my house right before my unexpected encounter with Erma. After we talked to Joan, I called Tobin about doing some work for me. It took some prodding, but finally he really unloaded about Cosette."

"You're going to have Tobin do work for you?" asked Miles. His eyebrows raised in alarm. "Won't that make

Dusty mad? I thought your whole existence was tailored around keeping Dusty happy."

"That's why I put up with the ridiculous Puddin as my housekeeper. That's why I don't complain when he misses spots when he mows…that's right. He's the only yardman in town who will weed trim around my gnomes. I can't afford to make him upset," said Myrtle. "But I found out that Tobin does tree removal. He came over to take a look at my ailing pine tree down the hill."

Miles puckered his brow. "I don't remember a sick pine tree in your yard."

Myrtle pointed out the window. "Out by the lake."

Miles stood up to peer out the window. "The skinny one on the lakeshore? You're not spending good money to take it down, are you? It'll fall in the lake eventually. Simply because you wanted to talk to Tobin?"

"I called for an estimate, that's all. The only problem is that he gave me such a good price on it that he'll probably keep bugging me to have it removed."

Miles glanced idly back at the kitchen window and jumped. "That animal. It's really a holy terror, Myrtle. Can't you do something about it?"

Myrtle turned to see Pasha glaring ominously at Miles. "She just doesn't like you, Miles. You give her mean looks and call her *that animal*. She's an absolute love with me. And what I don't understand is that people keep telling me that I should leave Pasha alone because she's a wild creature…and then they'll tell me that I should do something about her. Very contradictory."

"I suppose we mean that you've got some sort of obligation to the animal. Seeing as how you're feeding her and everything," said Miles stiffly.

"I had her spayed and she's had all her shots. However, I'm not exactly planning on taking Pasha to a cat psychologist to find out why she dislikes most human beings on this planet except for me. I simply accept that she has her reasons. She's a very clever feline," said Myrtle.

Pasha bared her teeth at Miles.

"Very disconcerting," said Miles grouchily.

Chapter Nine

There was a jaunty rap at the front door and Myrtle cursed under her breath. "It's Joan. And it looks like I've babysat by plopping the kids in front of the television the whole time." She pushed herself out of the chair and grabbed her cane.

"You did do that," said Miles. "But it was so much better than the alternative. And we didn't even have to boot up your computer."

Joan looked even jollier than she had when she'd been dropping off Noah. She greeted Myrtle and Miles with a huge smile on her face. Myrtle was surprised to see that she had dimples—she'd never smiled enough for Myrtle to see them. Her mother's demise seemed to put her in an extraordinarily good mood. "How was Noah?" she asked, then spotted him staring with fascination at the television screen.

Myrtle said quickly, "Oh, we had a great time. Yes. We had snacks and we colored pictures, and I mentioned French to him, and…." She trailed off and winced as Noah continued watching, totally engrossed on the screen without sparing his mother a glance. "We turned on the television. Miles came over and he and I visited while the boys watched a cartoon. I hope that's all right," she finished meekly.

"It's absolutely fine," said Joan, eyes twinkling behind her thick glasses. She started putting Noah's toys back in the basket she'd brought over.

"Is it?" asked Myrtle. "For some reason, I'd gotten the impression that Noah was always expanding his intellectual horizons in ways that a cartoon dinosaur couldn't provide."

The dinosaur on the television appeared to be putting on the wrong outfit every day of the week. If it were snowing outside, he wore a bathing suit. If it were sweltering, he wore a winter coat. Myrtle supposed this could potentially be considered educational. In a very meager way.

Joan rolled her eyes. "That was Mother's idea. Poor Noah hasn't had a minute of unscheduled time since he was able to sit up by himself. Mother paid for foreign language teachers and music classes and sports coaches. He's probably absorbed in the TV because he's never seen anything like it before." Joan's entire posture changed as she spoke about her mother. She slumped and her shoulders hunched over as if she were trying to hide.

"How did everything go at your dad's house?" asked Miles. "Is he doing any better?"

"And is your aunt still there?" asked Myrtle, trying to look sweetly concerned, when in fact she wanted to see if her chances were any better for speaking directly to Lucas."

"Aunt Hazel is still there, yes. She's going to stay until a couple of days after the funeral to help out. And it went really well, Miles, thanks. Hard, of course, to go through Mother's things, but it went well. Dad kept asking me if I wanted Mother's things and I had to keep turning him down…but that was the only real issue," said Joan. She snorted. "As if Mother and I were the same size. Mother was as skinny as they come. And I…" She motioned to the rolls of fat showing over her sweatpants.

"Well, I'm sure there are plenty of charities that will love to take her clothes," said Myrtle.

"Exactly." Joan brooded for a minute, obviously still thinking about her mother. "We were different sizes. We had different temperaments. Different personalities. I don't especially want to have reminders of Mother all over my house. I'm very sorry she's gone," said Joan, not really sounding at all sorry. "But I know the charities will be delighted to have her things. And we got so much done. It will be good for Dad not to have to live around all Mother's things…he'll feel a lot more at peace there."

Myrtle thought this was an odd way of phrasing it. "Well, you're certainly good to help him out. I know he probably isn't sleeping real well and isn't sure which way is up."

Joan said, "Yes, but Aunt Hazel is helping out a lot, too. The funeral is on for tomorrow, by the way. Aunt Hazel wrote up the obituary—a good thing, since I had no idea what to say about Mother. And she's helping tidy the house up for any guests who might come by after the funeral or to drop in beforehand. Dad's getting to the point where he can at least talk to visitors now. Thank goodness, Aunt Hazel has been here. Now all he has to do is deal with the life insurance company and business-related things like that."

Myrtle saw Miles raise his eyebrows at her. Myrtle said carefully, "Well, I'll be the first to admit that there can be a comfort in money—funerals are expensive things, aren't they?"

"Exactly. And Mother and Dad were flat out of money anyway, so thank goodness for the life insurance policy. And for such a big one—Dad will be completely out of the hole."

"How very modern of your father! He's so right to realize that even women who stay at home are of great value. Smart of him to get a policy to recognize that," said Myrtle.

"Dad said that Mother was such a valuable part of their home that he'd have to hire a team of professionals to do all the things she did. Mother bragged about it. He found her so valuable that he took out a large life insurance policy on her. He'd have to have a gardener, a housekeeper and more, just to replace all that she did. Of course, this policy covers hiring for those areas—and more."

Noah finally pulled himself away from the television and sleepily put his arms around her, nuzzling his head against her leg.

"Looks like Noah has gotten sleepy. Even better! I should bring him by more often. Now he can have a nap and I can get things done at my own house. Thanks so much for having him over."

After Joan left with Noah and the basket of toys, Myrtle and Miles discovered that Jack had fallen asleep. He was a small heap on the floor in front of the television set. "Elaine will be here in another fifteen minutes," she said. "Tell me what you think about this life insurance policy."

"Maybe it explains the connection between Felix and the Whitlows?" asked Miles. "After all, Felix sells life insurance policies. Maybe it was only business the whole time."

"But that doesn't explain why Sybil would have been so mad at Cosette. If anything, it seems like she should have been *nicer* to Cosette, especially with a business connection between her boyfriend and Cosette's husband."

Miles said, "That's true. It also seems sort of odd that Lucas would have a large policy on Cosette. That's not to say that she didn't play a vital role in their family, just that she wasn't a breadwinner at all. Usually people want life insurance policies to help replace lost income. Unless maybe they got large policies on each other—maybe Cosette had a matching one on Lucas."

"Right. I have a feeling the police are going to find it all rather peculiar, too. And Lucas might become even more of a suspect. I'm sure the police already know. I do need to talk with Felix," said Myrtle, mulling it over. "With the funeral tomorrow, though, I'll have to set an appointment with him for the day after."

Miles said doubtfully, "Do you think he'll disclose who he sold policies to? Isn't there some sort of confidentiality agreement?"

"You're getting confused with priests and doctors. Besides, I'm sure I can probably trick the information out of him. People always underestimate me, and think I'm such a harmless biddy. You wouldn't believe the things relative strangers tell me sometimes. I'm sure I can get him to tell me who had policies and why Lucas would have had such a large policy on Cosette."

Myrtle decided later that she should have realized there was some sort of curse on her the moment she woke up the next morning and pulled a muscle in her shoulder, merely by getting out of the bed. Getting old was most vexing.

She took two ibuprofen and continued getting ready. There was a funeral to attend and a story to write. And it was going to be a *good* story. Much better than that cub reporter's. She stopped short in the process of dressing. She'd told Sloan she'd send in that silly helpful tips column last night and she'd completely forgotten.

Myrtle hurried into the living room and plopped down at her desk, pulling up her email on her computer. She came up with a column, keeping it in her usual jaunty-tip-column-voice. The only problem was the tips. She couldn't for the life of her think up any new tips—the only ones that popped into her head were the ones she'd used in past columns. She stared at the computer in desperation, knowing she needed to get ready for the funeral. An odd pawing sound distracted her for a moment and she walked into the kitchen to see what was making the noise.

Pasha was pawing fervently at the kitchen window. Myrtle absently opened it. "Here, kitty," she said, still thinking about the tips. She pulled out some canned food from the pantry, not realizing until later that she was giving Pasha premium canned salmon.

By the time she sat back down at the computer, she'd decided that she would most certainly have to make her tips up. She'd figured she'd have to do that anyway. Myrtle wasn't feeling the slightest bit creative, so she decided to use old superstitions as tips. "Don't open your umbrella indoors." "Don't walk under open ladders." "Breaking mirrors is bad luck." She glanced over it to proofread and shook her head. Sloan was really going to think she had dementia. So would half the town! But she was past deadline. If Sloan decided she and the helpful tip column were through, then she could make the case for being a regular reporter. Say that the tip column was too boring for her and she needed something more stimulating.

Myrtle hurried off again to the bedroom, still in her slip, with Pasha following her. She needed to find her funeral dress. Church had become so relaxed that the times she did attend, she wore black slacks. The only time she really wore a dress anymore was at funerals and there was only one particularly solemn dress that fit the bill. But where was it? She knew she'd worn it a couple of months ago for two hours at Mabel Iverson's funeral.

Myrtle pushed hanging blouses and slacks around vigorously, looking for the dour dress while Pasha settled on Myrtle's bed, on top of the pantyhose she'd set out to wear. Finally, Myrtle discovered the dress and yanked it out of the closet. She stared at the garment. Had she *eaten* after Mabel's funeral? She certainly couldn't recall having eaten afterward. And yet, there appeared to be a large—no, actually, a *giant*—stain of what very well could be gravy on the front of the dress.

Since this was The Funeral Dress, Myrtle held it up against her and frowned critically at her image in the mirror.

Was this dark, squiggling stain noticeable? Maybe she was standing in a sunbeam and it was more noticeable than if she were standing in the shade. Except that it was a bright, sunny day and the stupid stain would probably stand out like a neon sign.

Myrtle turned and spotted Pasha, happily kneading her stockings into pilled shreds. She closed her eyes. All right. These were clearly signs she wouldn't be wearing her funeral dress today. What else did she have? She pushed through the clothes and found a pair of appropriately somber black pants and a black and white checked jacket. She sighed. It must be a hundred degrees out there, but she felt as though she shouldn't have bare arms at a funeral. That was another reason her funeral dress was so perfect—it had three-quarter length sleeves.

She looked at the clock. Now she was running late, and she never ran late. She pulled off the slip, dressed, and shoved her black flats on. She powdered her nose, combed her white hair so that it wasn't standing up like Einstein's, and rummaged around for her lipstick. Where on earth was her lipstick? Her pulled muscle was throbbing now as she frantically searched for the lipstick. She *had* to find it. At this point, she was so pale and washed-out, they'd likely mistake her for the corpse and pitch her into the grave instead of Cosette.

There was no lipstick in the drawer so she tried to retrace her steps from yesterday. Hadn't she reapplied the lipstick before Elaine picked up Jack? Because she wanted to look fresh and rested and perfectly capable of looking after two preschool boys by herself? Where had she put the lipstick? And why did she only have the one tube left?

Myrtle's eyes opened wide and she hurried to the laundry room and pulled open the dryer door. Sure enough—there was the lipstick. Or, what was left of it, considering it had melted and dried all over the load of laundry that she'd run.

Now muttering imprecations under her breath, she gave up on the idea of looking like a living person and grabbed her cane. It wasn't a long walk, but since she was running late, it was unfortunate that she had to walk at all. She opened the front door and saw a mangled rabbit on the front step. Myrtle blinked at it as Pasha bounded past her from inside the house, then turned to look at Myrtle as if encouraging her to enjoy the gift she'd provided her.

The carcass would clearly have to be dealt with later, decided Myrtle as she locked the door behind her and hurried off.

Myrtle hadn't gone far down the sidewalk when she heard a car approach and a voice call dryly, "Going my way?"

It was Miles. "Thank goodness you're here," she muttered, crossing in front of the car to get into the passenger seat.

"That's the second time this week that I've heard those words from you," said Miles. "Is this the end of times?"

Myrtle ignored him, distracted by the condition of her black slacks. "What on earth? I have Pasha fur all over my pants!" She swiped at the fur, trying unsuccessfully to brush it off, resorting finally to picking at it.

"Having a rough day?" asked Miles.

"I'll say. And now I'm on my way to a funeral, so the day isn't likely to improve."

"Remind me again what you're hoping to accomplish by attending this funeral. Is it Felix you're trying to speak with?" asked Miles.

"No, I've made an appointment to see him at his office. I can't imagine he'll be at Cosette's funeral anyway. I'm mostly curious to see if I can pick up any clues there. Maybe

I can hear from Joan or Lucas. Or who knows—maybe Sybil will show up."

"Sybil? Why? To grieve?" Miles sounded dubious.

"To make sure Cosette is dead," said Myrtle, moving her cane to the side so she could stretch out. She kept pawing at her slacks to get the cat fur off.

Miles glanced over, before glancing back at the road. "I don't mean to make you feel bad, Myrtle, but is everything okay? You don't seem as—together—as you usually do."

"Don't I? That's just because it's the worst day ever. It's a wonder I'm even able to get to the funeral, as messed up as today has been so far," said Myrtle.

At that moment, on cue, Miles' car started making a terrible, jarring bumping. He abruptly pulled to the side of the little tree-lined street, parked, and got out. He appeared to be making some ungentlemanly comments to his car, then crossed around again and got back into the driver's seat. "Could someone possibly have put a curse on you today? I have a flat."

"What? No! We're nearly there. Can't you drive on the rim?"

"No ma'am, I can't. It will do all kinds of damage to the rim. I wouldn't have enough control of the car's direction, and driving on the rim could even spark a fire," said Miles firmly. "We'll walk the rest of the way. I'll assist you."

"I don't need assistance," said Myrtle sullenly. "The air conditioning in the car was an added bonus—and I'd have gotten to the funeral more quickly. That's the reason I wanted to ride."

"And I thought it was my scintillating conversation," said Miles. "Well, there's nothing else to be done. Let's walk over."

By the time they'd arrived at the cemetery, the sun was high in the sky. There was no wind, not even the tiniest breeze, and the air was dripping with humidity. The black and white blouse was sticking to Myrtle as was Miles' button-down shirt to him.

"I thought old people didn't perspire," grumbled Myrtle.

"I don't think they say *that.* They only say we don't perspire enough to keep from getting heat stroke." The words came out in panting breaths and he took off his jacket and folded it over his arm as they walked.

"Oh pooh. Look, the service has already started," said Myrtle, stopping short.

Sure enough, the minister was speaking to the assembled mourners, holding a Bible and somehow looking cool as a cucumber despite the robes he was wearing.

"They won't mind if we walk up and stand at the edge of the mourners," said Miles. "It's not as if we're trying to find a seat under the funeral home tent."

However, Myrtle felt, what was, for her, an unusual reticence. "I don't think so. Everyone will turn around, and I don't want people irritated with me if I'm trying to pump them for information later." Besides, she looked horrid. Even Cosette would look better than she did this morning.

"Pooh," muttered Myrtle again. "Here comes Sloan."

Miles raised his eyebrows at her. "I thought you liked Sloan. Or liked working with him at the paper, anyway."

"I forgot about the dumb tips column and had to throw something together. I emailed it to him right before I left, so he won't have known that I sent anything in. He's probably coming to ask me about it."

Miles said, "This will be entertaining. He's obviously still completely intimidated by you because of bad classroom memories. I can't imagine him fussing at you about missing a deadline."

"Well, that paper is his baby. I think he'll muster up the gumption to fuss." Sloan hurried up and got into whispering distance from them, since the funeral was going on mere yards away.

Myrtle decided a preemptive strike was in order. "I emailed you the column," she hissed at him. "I sent it before I left, so you haven't gotten it yet, that's all."

Sloan's face was beaming. "Oh, I got it already. On my phone."

Myrtle sighed. She had a cell phone, but she used it for phone calls only. It always surprised her that people received emails on their phones. And it irritated her to be surprised. "All right. Well, I know the column wasn't full of my usual helpful tips." She certainly hoped she got fired from the helpful hints column for her transgressions—and transferred to what passed for a news bureau.

"It sure wasn't. But it was brilliant!"

Now Myrtle squinted at him. Was *Sloan* becoming demented?

"You know," said Sloan. "Because tomorrow is Friday the Thirteenth. You put together a really clever column! All those old superstitions. It was a stroke of genius."

Maybe it was subconscious genius, but Myrtle doubted it.

"Glad you liked it," she said grudgingly. "And if you liked that, you'll really like the investigative article I'm writing for you." She suddenly felt as if he might need a reminder that she was indeed writing such an article.

"Oh. Oh, I thought somehow we'd settled that, Miss Myrtle. Kim, remember me talking about Kim? She's my intern. She's here right now actually, getting the scoop on the funeral. That's her in the back row under the tent." He gestured with a fat finger to an attractive young woman wearing an impeccable and rather snug-fitting black suit with heels and large sunglasses.

Myrtle seethed that the girl was not only there reporting but had gotten there in enough time to sit near the relatives under the tent. And that she didn't appear to have any stains on her funeral dress. She likely didn't have any melted lipstick in her dryer, either. Perhaps she even took all her clothes to a dry cleaner—she looked like that type of girl.

Kim was already not Myrtle's favorite person.

"In my recollection we'd settled it differently, Sloan. Your intern was going to do all the basic stories and I'd provide more in-depth coverage. As a senior reporter," said Myrtle. That was perhaps a stretch. But she was a senior. And she was a reporter.

Sloan looked doubtful. "Kim is actually doing all the news coverage related to the murder, Miss Myrtle. But if you want to come up with a story of some kind, I'm sure I could squeeze it in." He glanced at his watch. "The service should be finishing up in a minute. If you have some time afterward, I'd be happy to introduce you to her."

Myrtle thought she'd pass. Sloan gave them a jolly wave, which seemed a bit out of place at a funeral, and walked to the outer edge of the group of mourners.

"Great. Now here comes Red. My day just keeps getting better and better," said Myrtle. "All the people I want to talk to aren't coming over and I'm surrounded by people I'd rather avoid."

Miles chuckled as Red came up.

"Kind of late aren't you, Mama?" asked Red. He leaned closer to her, peering at her clothes. "Where is your funeral dress? You're wearing slacks to a funeral? That's not like you."

"Apparently, I had a lot of drippy gravy after Mabel Iverson's funeral a couple of months ago," said Myrtle, still irritated at the memory. "That was such a short service and reception that I think I figured I could just hang the dress back up and wear it again. But no—gravy all down the front."

"Where's your lipstick?" asked Red, frowning.

"Melted at the bottom of my dryer. Want to do your good deed for the day and clean it up for me?"

"No thanks," he said. "I'm doing my good deed for the day by coming to Cosette's funeral."

Myrtle glanced at the mourners. "Trying to see if one of the assembled has a terribly guilty visage? Or looks a bit too gleeful?"

"It's usually not that easy," said Red dryly. "I'm just keeping an eye on things. And now the service is ending, so I need to go." He stopped for a moment. "By the way, I met the new reporter that Sloan hired. She seems to be a real go-getter. Have you met her?"

"He hasn't *hired* her. She's an intern. And a mere infant. No, I haven't met her." His words irritated her and she looked away from him into the woods. She frowned. "I thought the body was supposed to be in the casket," she said, squinting at the woods.

Chapter Ten

Red sighed. "The body *is* in the casket, Mama."

"Then what's that over there?" she asked, pointing over at the woods.

"Probably a makeshift camp that teens set up to do some drinking on the sly. Look, I've got to go." He hurried off toward the group standing around the grave.

"Miles," said Myrtle. "That doesn't look like a makeshift camp to me."

Miles said, "I don't know. It could be a balled-up sleeping bag, I guess." He looked at Myrtle. "Why do I have the feeling we're going to investigate this lump in the woods?"

"Because you know I'm a better sleuth than Red," said Myrtle with certainty. She held tightly to her cane and started moving in the direction of the woods.

"Myrtle," said Miles, "here comes Sloan and that young reporter. I think they're coming to talk to you."

Myrtle groaned and turned back around. "I need to redirect them. Just in case that's a body over there. All I need is Miss Hot Shot horning in." She pasted a smile on her face as Sloan and the young woman walked up.

The hot day was getting to Sloan and his face had rivulets of perspiration coursing down it. "Kim, I wanted to introduce you to Miss Myrtle. She's the matriarch of Bradley, North Carolina, and the top source of information and leads. She's taught English to most of the adults in this town."

"Whether they wanted to learn English or not," said Myrtle with a nod. She beamed at Kim, who was a very attractive young woman with blonde hair and smart clothes.

Her eyes had a gleam of intelligence…and also, thought Myrtle, of condescension.

"It's good to meet you," murmured Kim with a small smile. But her gaze restlessly roamed the crowd as if she wished she were anywhere else but talking to this particular old lady at this particular funeral.

"As a matter of fact," said Myrtle, "I do have a lead for you, just as Sloan said."

Kim perked up and refocused her attention on Myrtle. "Do you?"

"I sure do. I always want to help a fellow reporter," said Myrtle nobly.

Miles, overcome by a sudden coughing fit, stepped away.

"Do you see that woman over there? The one who is heading toward the parking lot? She's got sort of a rodent-like face? Her name is Erma Sherman. She has an interesting angle on the case that I think you'll want to hear about."

Kim was already walking away toward Erma when Myrtle said, "Just keep digging deeper, dear! She has many different stories to relate." Mostly about her ingrown toenails and digestive complaints. And Erma was impossible to get away from. That should keep Kim busy.

"I'll take her out for coffee," said Kim to Sloan. "Can I expense that out?"

Sloan looked a little sad and said, "Sure. What's the price of a couple of coffees compared to great journalism?" He gave Myrtle a salute. "Thanks for that!"

Myrtle smiled at him. "Oh, you're very welcome." She watched as Sloan walked off to talk to Lucas Whitlow—who appeared to be barely keeping it together.

Miles came back over to join Myrtle, eyes watering. "For heaven's sake," Myrtle said crossly, "it wasn't all that funny."

"You were such a Lady Bountiful, bestowing leads to junior reporters," said Miles, wheezing a bit.

"And Miss Kim deserved every bit of it. I saw that belittling attitude. She deserves every awful description of every disgusting malady that Erma Sherman has. Come on, let's check out this campsite thing," said Myrtle, thumping away with her cane toward the woods.

Miles hurried along beside her. "I thought we needed to try to talk to Lucas and Joan. Or see if Sybil or Felix were here. Or Tobin."

Myrtle kept moving forward until she got to the lump on the ground, shaded in the shadows of the trees. "Tobin is here, all right. But I don't believe we're going to be able to do any talking with him. I believe he's dead."

Tobin was indeed dead. He appeared to have been clubbed with a nearby shovel.

Myrtle said sadly, "You know, Tobin was a fairly likeable guy. Hard-worker. Concerned about our street. And he gave me such a good price on taking down that pine tree." She frowned. "He was something of a pine tree himself. Tall guy—he must have been kneeling to do some weeding for someone to have hit him like that."

"Nice eulogy, Myrtle. Now we need to tell Red," said Miles.

"With pleasure," muttered Myrtle.

"Myrtle!"

"I don't mean that I'm taking pleasure in poor Tobin's death! Just in the fact that Red was pooh-poohing me about anything being in the woods…*mistakenly* pooh-poohing me." She gazed in the direction of the oblivious mourners. "You know, I kind of hate ruining the service to report a murder."

"The service is over. It was apparently lovely. Everyone looks very touched. But Red needs to talk to potential witnesses, so we must stop everyone from leaving." Miles seemed very insistent on this point, and dashed across the cemetery.

Myrtle waited where she was, gazing down at the body. It looked as if Tobin might have been doing some yard work here. Not only was the shovel nearby, but there were also some hedge-clippers and a dark plastic trash bag close to the body. She didn't spot any other clues. Had Tobin come to the graveyard early to spruce things up and someone followed him here? Had he known something that the murderer wanted to keep quiet?

Myrtle looked up as she heard Red's voice calling out to everyone across the cemetery. "I'm sorry, but if everyone would stay put and remain where you are. Please don't leave yet." He was pulling out his phone, probably to call the state police, and striding quickly toward her.

"Body?" he asked her, a little breathlessly and without looking her directly in the eye.

"Body," she said with certainty. "Tobin Tinker, as a matter of fact. Poor fellow. Looks as if he was out here doing some work."

"Tobin does yard maintenance for the church," said Red absently. Then, "All right, Mama. Sorry I didn't pay attention to you earlier. But it did sound completely preposterous, you know."

"Perhaps it did. But you should know I'd know a body when I am looking at one. Especially at this point."

Red said, "Yes. Although how we got to this point is quite baffling to me. Okay, you know the drill. Back away from the body now. I've got a forensics team on its way and I'll need to speak with folks here at the cemetery."

Myrtle wanted to speak to folks at the cemetery, too. Fortunately, she had lots of opportunity to do so since Red was so busy trying to contain the crime scene, keep folks away from the body, and talk on his phone at the same time.

Everyone stood in a semicircle around the woods, gaping at Red. Lucas was the only one who wasn't particularly interested in the goings-on at this end of the grounds. He was still standing near Cosette's grave, blinking in confusion, and favoring his good leg as if his other knee was bothering him. His thick, gray hair blew about in the humid breeze. He was wearing an old suit that Myrtle could tell had frayed around the wrists. He looked more like an absent-minded professor than an accountant.

Myrtle walked up to him. "Lucas, I wanted to say again how sorry I am about Cosette."

Lucas stared vacantly at her. Myrtle wondered if maybe he were on medication. She tried again, "The service was lovely. I know it's exactly what Cosette would have wanted."

These words seemed to work a bit better. Lucas stirred out of his reverie and said, "Do you think so? I hoped she would have. Hazel helped a lot, you know." He looked vaguely around again. "Where did Hazel go?"

Myrtle spotted her in the crowd. "She's down the hill near the woods."

Lucas frowned as the situation unfolding below them finally registered. "What's going on down there? Did someone get sick?"

"I'm afraid there's been another tragic death," said Myrtle. She shook her head sadly. "I don't know what the world's coming to."

"Another death? Who is it?" Lucas clutched a hand on the top of one of the nearby chairs under the funeral home tent.

"Your neighbor, Tobin. I know he lives across the street from you—were y'all close?" asked Myrtle innocently.

Lucas looked at her, and then rapidly glanced away. "Oh, that's too bad...he was always a good neighbor. No, I'm afraid we weren't very close. He was often at odds with Cosette for having so many events at our house. The cars blocked his driveway, you see. But he and I got along well. Tobin actually came over to express his condolences."

"And you talked to him?" asked Myrtle, remembering that Lucas was barricaded in a bedroom, at least when she'd been there with Miles.

"Only for a few minutes," said Lucas. "I wanted to make sure he knew I had no hard feelings about the problems he'd had with Cosette. And he seemed to want to patch things up with me, not that I'd had any problems with him. We let bygones be bygones."

His gaze wandered back to the group at the edge of the woods. "What is Red saying about Tobin's death? Does it seem to be a heart attack? It's so hot here that I'd think even a heat stroke is a possibility." Always polite, he added, "I'm so sorry about the weather, Miss Myrtle. It was kind of you to come out in the heat like this."

Myrtle said, "I was happy to, Lucas. But unfortunately, it does seem to be another murder. I noticed that he'd been struck over the head with a shovel. I know you saw Tobin the other day when he came by your house, but have you seen him more recently than that? This morning, maybe?"

Lucas shook his head, again not meeting Myrtle's eyes. At that moment Red walked up, saying, "Lucas, if you don't mind, could I speak with you for a few minutes?"

Joan walked up, wearing black pants that were too tight on her and a similarly ill-fitting blouse. Her eyes behind her thick glasses were concerned. "Why do you need to speak with Dad?"

"I need to speak to everyone here to try to figure out Tobin's movements, Joan," said Red steadily. This time Red gave his mother a beseeching look and she was only too happy to comply.

"Joan, it's okay. Red has to talk to everybody. Unfortunately, there's been another dreadful murder. That's what's happening down near the woods. Tobin Tinker is dead."

"What?" Joan gasped. "But I just saw him! I saw him this morning at ten o'clock when I was on my way to take Noah to Elaine's house. He was as alive as anything—doing yard work here at the church."

"Did you see anyone else around while you were driving around?"

Joan said slowly, "You know, I did see something a little unusual. I saw Felix Nelson walking by. I don't think of him as someone who exercises. He didn't look like he was walking for his health, either—he had a suit on and that bow tie of his. I chuckled over it, actually. He looked like he was off for a business meeting instead of a walk. It was already hot and he was sweating. I figured Felix couldn't stop being formal, even when he was working out."

Joan looked toward the woods again. "I understand why someone would want to murder my mother, but why on earth would someone want to murder Tobin Tinker?"

Myrtle watched the other mourners while she waited for Red to talk with her. The sun was nearing its hottest point of the day, but it was ignored by the funeral-goers, who were avidly watching as a forensics team arrived and as Red spoke to various people at the funeral.

Myrtle was at the point in her life where heat was not something to be ignored or trifled with. She'd seated herself under the funeral home tent as soon as she'd spoken with Joan. Miles spotted her and turned from the conversation he was having with four widows (Miles was extremely popular among the widow population) to join her. The widows shot Myrtle a look.

"Red seems to be talking to everyone pretty quickly," said Miles. "I'm hoping we can all get out of here soon. I'm burning up." He removed his suit jacket, carefully folding it over his arm.

"He's just finding out what they were doing this morning and if they saw Tobin," said Myrtle with a shrug. "It wouldn't take too long to work through most of the people here." She squinted at a point near the road. "Isn't that Sybil down there? It's got to be. No one else in town drives a 1970s Chevy Caprice."

Miles leaned forward in his folding chair. "That's Sybil all right. She wasn't at the funeral though, was she? She was probably driving past and noticed that everyone was gathered around the woods instead of around the graveside and wanted to see what was going on."

"Or else she murdered Tobin Tinker for knowing too much and is inexorably drawn to the scene of the crime," muttered Myrtle, watching Sybil. "Joan has already mentioned to me that she saw Felix this morning."

"Doing what? Murdering Tobin?" Miles sounded startled.

"No. Well, not as far as we know. She saw him walking nearby—in a suit."

"Maybe he's had the kind of day I've had. Maybe he had a flat and had to walk over to a business meeting."

Myrtle made a scoffing noise. "More than one flat tire in a day? Don't' you think that's kind of unlikely?"

"Not particularly. Maybe there are a few nails in the road and he and I were both unlucky enough to drive over them. I'm simply pointing out that Felix wasn't seen beating Tobin Tinker over the head with a shovel—he was merely seen walking near the cemetery in a suit."

"Joan said that she saw Tobin alive at ten o'clock this morning. Her alibi is apparently Elaine—she dropped Noah off with Elaine before coming to the service. I guess they must have visited for a while. If she saw Tobin then, that must have been right before he was killed—the service started at eleven," said Myrtle.

"What was Lucas doing at ten?" asked Miles.

"Red asked him that after he finished talking with Joan. Lucas was getting ready for the service. He said that Hazel could vouch for him," said Myrtle. "But I doubt that Hazel was with him the entire morning. She had to get ready herself. It seems to me that it would have been easy enough for Lucas to hop in the car, drive to the cemetery, murder Tobin, and drive back home."

"Maybe. But after ten? Could he have done it after ten? That would have been right before the service started—he probably had to arrive early, too. It sounds like a really risky thing for him to have done," said Miles.

"Maybe Joan isn't telling the truth," said Myrtle. "She could be covering for herself or her father. Tobin could have been dead at nine a.m., for all we know."

"Forensics would have a more accurate idea of the window for the murder," said Miles in a hopeful voice. "Perhaps Red will share that information with us when it becomes available."

"And pigs might fly," said Myrtle.

Miles and Myrtle sat quietly for a few minutes, hoping for a breeze.

"How are we going to get back home, by the way? I'd forgotten your car is out of commission," said Myrtle.

"The same way we got here, I guess. We'll walk. Once we reach my car, though, I need to stop and change the tire real quick."

"I need to find a ride," said Myrtle. "It must be over one hundred degrees now. I've been out in the heat long enough without pushing it." An idea occurred to her. "I know. I'll ask Sybil for a ride, since she's suddenly on the scene. That'll give me the chance to ask her a few questions, too."

Miles said, "Questions? I thought you were going to talk with her under the guise of getting her opinion on book club picks. Besides, Sybil is skulking around like she doesn't want to be seen. She couldn't be happy with you coming up and asking her for a ride." He clearly was proud of his book club idea and didn't want Myrtle to give up on it.

"Well, if the perfect opportunity to ask Sybil some questions pops up, it seems like I should go ahead and use it," said Myrtle. She glanced away from Miles and back toward the street. "Shoot. Never mind, she's gone. Maybe Red can take me back."

"There's no way. He'll be stuck here with the state police for hours," said Miles.

Another car pulled up to see what was going on in the cemetery woods. It was a disreputable-looking older model American car.

Myrtle perked up. "Look! It's Puddin and Dusty." She clapped her hands together.

"Now, that's a first. I've never heard you mention your housekeeper and yardman with such excitement before."

"I'm sure they can give me a ride…it should be my house that they're on the way over to. It certainly should be! Puddin hasn't cleaned for ages and the dust bunnies are chasing each other through the house. My yard could use a touch-up, too."

Myrtle grabbed her cane and hurried toward Puddin and Dusty's car before they took off like Sybil had.

Chapter Eleven

"Wait!" called Miles. "What about Red? Doesn't he need to talk to you?"

"He knows where to find me," called back Myrtle without turning around.

Puddin and Dusty didn't exactly look pleased to see her, but they never did. Puddin was a pale, dumpy woman who avoided housework whenever a shortcut presented itself. Dusty was actually a half-decent yardman, but it was difficult to get him to regularly come by the house. Together…they were the best Myrtle could do.

Puddin appeared to be eating a fig and the juice was running unchecked down her chin. "Need a ride?" she reluctantly asked. "Dusty and me was going to your house just now."

"Yes, Miles brought me, but he has a flat and it's too hot for me to walk back," Myrtle climbed into the backseat, pushing aside a laundry basket full of cleaning supplies as she did. She glowered at the supplies, which all appeared untouched and brand-new. Puddin was fond of using up the homeowner's cleaners instead of her own.

"What's going on up there?" asked Dusty, bobbing his head to indicate the throng of mourners near the woods.

"A murder," said Myrtle, scowling at her black pants. Did she still have that much cat fur on them? It looked as if she were wearing a pair of angora slacks.

Dusty nodded as if that were a perfectly reasonable and acceptable explanation.

"Who of?" asked Puddin, turning around to look at Myrtle. Her piggy eyes squinted at her.

"Tobin Tinker," said Myrtle.

Dusty grunted. "More business for me, then."

Myrtle felt, but didn't say, that people who had gotten used to Tobin's level of competence and expertise wouldn't be particularly interested in hiring Dusty to help them with yard work.

Neither Puddin nor Dusty seemed inclined to inquire any more about the murder. They pulled up into Myrtle's driveway and Puddin calmly wrapped the rest of her fig in a napkin.

"Where do you get your figs?" asked Myrtle.

"My backyard."

"How'd you keep the birds and squirrels and ants away from those figs, Puddin?"

"They'd have to fight me for them," said Puddin simply.

Dusty had an ancient lawnmower in the trailer behind the car. He rolled it out while Puddin waited for Myrtle to fish her keys from her purse. "Sure is a lot easier mowin' yer lawn with no gnomes sittin' in the middle of everything," he observed.

Myrtle was sure that it was. However, she wanted to reserve the right to pull gnomes out of her little storage building whenever she wanted. "Just remember we have a deal where you weed-trim whenever they are out there. Red's been behaving lately, so I haven't had to drag out the gnomes in protest. That could change at any time."

Dusty shrugged. "It's yer property." The tone intimated that there would never be gnomes of any sort on Dusty's own lawn.

Myrtle glanced at her doorstep. "By the way, Puddin, there's a corpse on the front step that you'll need to dispose of. I guess just put it in a plastic grocery bag and toss it in my outside trash bin."

"What!" Puddin squinted at the front step. "That witch cat again."

"Nonsense. Your superstitions exhaust me, Puddin."

Myrtle finally fished her keys from her pocketbook, and she and Puddin walked inside, carefully stepping over the dead rabbit as they entered. "As you can see, there's dust everywhere. So I need you to dust first and then vacuum. The kitchen and bathroom could use a scrubbing, if you have time after that." She almost laughed as she said it. Puddin would not have time because it would take her fifteen minutes to even start. Ten minutes of that would be her getting the cleaning supplies ready. *Myrtle's* cleaning supplies.

"Got it," said Puddin in a singsong voice.

Puddin wasn't good for much. Myrtle had little hope that her home would be cleaner when she left. But sometimes she did furnish useful information. There was a real network among housekeepers in town and every single one of them loved to gossip. Puddin was apparently related in some respect to many of them. Puddin had long felt herself at a disadvantage when cleaning Myrtle's house since Myrtle no longer did anything that was gossip-worthy. If she ever had.

"As sort of a side note, what do you know about Sybil Brown or Felix Nelson?" asked Myrtle.

A pleased expression crossed Puddin's face and she immediately plopped down on Myrtle's sofa.

"No, no, Puddin. You can talk and dust at the same time."

"I was gonna vacuum first. Can't talk and vacuum. Your old machine is too noisy," said Puddin.

Myrtle gritted her teeth. "Then you should use your own vacuum. Besides, who vacuums *before* they dust? Doesn't make any sense. You're supposed to vacuum up the dust you've knocked to the floor."

Puddin ignored this. "Sybil and Felix. Let's see. Well, Sybil Brown doesn't have a cleaner. She's not real fancy, you know."

"*I'm* not fancy. I'm just old. Plenty of people who have housekeepers aren't fancy."

"Not her," said Puddin with satisfaction. She liked being right more than anything. She paused for effect, enjoying having Myrtle hang on her words. "Now that Felix. He has a cleaner for his office. Couldn't be bothered to clean it and mess up his nice suits."

"Do you clean his office?"

"No," drawled Puddin. "But my cousin Cee-Cee does. Twice a week she does."

Cee-Cee's work ethic was more evolved than Puddin's and she came from the harder-working branch of Puddin's family tree. Myrtle watched distastefully as Puddin made herself more comfortable on Myrtle's sofa, plumping a pillow behind her. She only hoped that Cousin Cee-Cee wasn't particularly discreet.

Apparently, she wasn't. "So Cee-Cee says that Sybil is always bugging Felix. Calls him up on the phone all the time, asking stupid stuff. What's his favorite color? What was the first pet he ever had? Drives him nuts. Sometimes he has Cee-Cee to answer the phone for him when he sees Sybil's number come up."

"Sounds like a good idea," muttered Myrtle. Who interrupts someone's workday with that kind of stuff?

"Right. Except then, Sybil got all green eyed over Cee-Cee. Thought Cee-Cee was too lovey-dovey with her Felix," said Puddin, sitting back on the sofa with satisfaction at Myrtle's surprise.

Myrtle *was* surprised. Because Cee-Cee, although somewhat better looking than the dumpy, dour Puddin, was nobody's pretty child. "Did Sybil *know* Cee-Cee? Did she think Cee-Cee was somebody else when she was picking up the phone?"

Puddin emphatically shook her head. "Nuh-uh. Because Cee-Cee cleans for Sybil's neighbor! She sees her every week."

So apparently, Sybil was simply delusional. She was so obsessed with Felix that she was jealous of *anyone* who spent time with him. Maybe Cosette wasn't having an affair with Felix. Maybe Sybil dreamed the whole thing up.

"Anything else?" asked Myrtle. "Maybe clients that Felix had? Did Cee-Cee ever mention seeing Cosette Whitlow at his office?"

Puddin looked bored again. She shrugged. "Who knows? Does anybody care? It's only an insurance company." She eyed the box of chocolates that Elaine had brought over to her as thanks for watching Jack.

Just then, Pasha made a joyful meow and bounded at Puddin. Pasha was especially attracted to anyone who was scared of her. Puddin shrieked and put her doughy hands up to block herself from the feline onslaught.

Pasha landed right on Puddin's knee, and started kneading her leg with her claws out as far as she could. Puddin howled and stood up to dump Pasha off her lap. "Witch!" she hissed at her. "She's a witch's cat."

"That foolishness again," said Myrtle with a snort, plucking Pasha off the floor and holding her protectively. "I'm grateful that Pasha helped move you off my sofa." She handed Puddin the duster and stroked Pasha lovingly.

Felix looked calmly and unsmilingly at Myrtle across the desk the next morning. "So you want to buy some life insurance, is that right?" He folded his hands together and watched Myrtle expectantly.

Myrtle said steadily, "I'm *considering* it, yes. For my loved ones. In the case of my sudden demise, you know."

She glanced around Felix's office. It was very tidy. Whether that was due to Puddin's cousin Cee-Cee or Felix's organization skills, she wasn't sure. He had only one piece of paper on his desk and a computer. The room was decorated sparsely with a fern on a stand in one corner, a file cabinet in another and a credenza. Myrtle noticed that Felix didn't seem to be very surprised at the fact that the octogenarian in front of him was interested in life insurance. She knew Miles would be wrong about that. A salesman was a salesman. While he was at it, he might try to sell her a dock in the desert, too.

"It's extremely wise of you to think about your survivors," Felix said smoothly in his pedantic manner. "After all, there are many things that a life insurance plan can pay for. Your final expenses for one thing."

Myrtle wrinkled her brow. Final expenses? Was there a toll road to heaven that she didn't know about? Then she realized he was referring to her funeral. "Oh, yes. My final expenses." Myrtle had a very matter-of-fact view toward funerals, which Felix wouldn't know. Hers was to be very simple, extremely cheap, and would involve cremation and a short memorial service at a later date. She hoped it would be the shortest, least-expensive funeral on record in Bradley, North Carolina. Myrtle had informed Red and Elaine that she would haunt them with a vengeance if they disregarded her wishes and turned her funeral into some elaborate affair.

She half-listened as Felix droned on about annuities, whole life insurance and policies. Surely, Cosette hadn't been interested in this man. He was about as lively and exciting as that fern in the corner. Oh, he was darkly handsome and meticulously dressed. He was certainly tidy. But his demeanor was stern and taciturn and not at all appealing. Sybil must be paranoid, just as Puddin was saying.

Myrtle interrupted him. “Yes, it *is* important to think about our loved ones, isn’t it? Because death can happen at any moment.”

Felix paused and blinked at the interruption. “Yes, it can. An excellent point, Mrs. Clover. As I was saying….”

“Just like poor Cosette Whitlow!” said Myrtle, opening her eyes wide and trying to look as much like a gossipy old woman as she possibly could.

He cleared his throat. “That’s right. Tragedies happen all the time.”

“You were there when it happened, weren’t you?” asked Myrtle. “At the drop-in that Cosette had.”

“No, not really. I don’t actually enjoy parties very much, so I avoid them as much as possible.”

“But I saw you there. At Cosette’s drop-in,” said Myrtle.

Felix sighed. “I really wasn’t *there*. I was only there for a moment. Then I left. I paid my respects to Cosette and Lucas, since they’re clients of mine.”

“Did Lucas and Cosette have policies through you, then?”

Felix said cautiously, “They were clients of mine, yes.”

“I know Lucas had a policy on Cosette. Did Cosette have one on Lucas?” She blinked innocently at Felix.

He studied Myrtle for a moment, fingering his bow tie, and then apparently judged her innocuous. Silly Felix.

“Cosette did not have one on Lucas. I think it was something they simply didn’t get around to,” said Felix. “The policy on Cosette was almost a compliment paid her by Lucas. To show how much value he placed on all she did at their home and in their community,” said Felix stiffly.

“Oh, I see,” said Myrtle. “Sort of a token gesture.”

“Not at all. It was a significant policy,” said Felix. “Everyone has different needs, you see. Now, moving on to *your* needs….”

Myrtle had absolutely no intention of purchasing any kind of a policy from Felix Nelson. But she didn't want to call this visit a total waste, either. She blinked coyly at Felix. "I hear that you and Sybil Brown are sweethearts," she said. "I think that's the cutest thing. Although I don't see any pictures of her in your office."

Felix sighed and appeared resigned to the fact that this generation, or at least Myrtle, needed to have some social conversation before jumping right into business discussions. "I don't think offices should showcase items of a personal nature," he said briskly. "Yes, Sybil and I spend time together. I'm not sure I'd define us as sweethearts." His mouth twisted when saying the word, as if it left a bitter taste in his mouth.

"That's not what I hear from Sybil," said Myrtle, taking on a surprised tone.

"Sybil knows exactly what the terms of our relationship are," said Felix firmly.

Myrtle wasn't at all sure that Felix was much of a catch. He seemed to find relationships one more thing to negotiate terms on. And he was far too complacent. She felt the need to shake things up.

"Were you having a quarrel there?" she asked in a concerned, tinkling voice that was nothing like her usual alto. "When I saw you, you certainly seemed angry. And so did Sybil. In fact…so did Cosette."

Felix stared silently at her for a couple of moments. He finally said coldly, "We were having a political discussion. We concurred that Congress was the real problem in this country. It made us all very angry as we discussed politics." He paused. "Very angry indeed."

Myrtle almost laughed out loud at the thought of Sybil engaging in political conversations, but she managed to bite her lip. "I see. Well, I'm certainly glad you didn't have a lover's quarrel. My." Felix was still looking quite frosty, so she added meekly, "Can you tell me more about planning for my final expenses?"

Felix's icy glare told her that he would be happy to arrange for her to need those final expenses sooner than she'd expected. She noticed how his fingers tightened around a large, glass paperweight on his desk as if he wished it were Myrtle's throat.

Chapter Twelve

Myrtle couldn't sleep that night, which she was certain had to do with Felix. Between his droning on about final expenses, the subject of murder, and Felix's clear displeasure with Myrtle, she was stuck with insomnia, but good.

She studied the light fixture on the ceiling, thinking for the millionth time that she really needed to change it out. Then she decided if she were coming up with home improvement projects for herself, then she really needed to get out of bed.

Most of the time, doing something very rote and boring would bore her back into the bed and to sleep. But after she'd worked for a few minutes trying to clean the mess out of her dryer (which Puddin conveniently had run out of time to do), she found she was just as awake. She knew she had one more *Tomorrow's Promise* to catch up on, but watching her soap opera was usually more of a stimulant than something to make her sleepy. She pulled the knitting needles and the yarn out of their bag and sat with them on her lap, looking down at them. Myrtle couldn't help it—she simply felt hopelessly clichéd with the knitting. *An old woman knitting away. Bah.*

She looked at the clock. Three o'clock. Myrtle decided that Miles was probably up. Then she hesitated. The last couple of times she'd bestowed a late-night visit on Miles, he hadn't been awake. Was he changing his sleeping patterns?

She found herself wavering about walking down to Miles's house, which made her sad. One of her favorite things was to share milk and cookies or a coffee with Miles when she couldn't sleep. But it appeared that she had worse insomnia these days than Miles had.

Myrtle jumped, as there was a knock on her front door. A murderer wouldn't knock though, surely. Politeness wasn't one of their virtues. She walked to the front door and peeped out the front window to make sure that there wasn't a frightening figure in a ski mask acting menacing on her front step.

She beamed. It was Miles. And for once, he wasn't meticulously dressed but appeared to have a navy-blue bathrobe on over a set of plaid pajamas.

"Miles!" She pulled the door open wide. "I was just thinking about coming over to visit you! But then I figured you'd be asleep and I'd wake you up as I have been doing lately."

Miles said, "On the other hand, I wasn't worried at all about coming by. Your insomnia has gotten so rampant that I knew you'd have to be awake. Naturally, if your lights were out I'd have simply turned around and gone back home."

Myrtle thought that he might be pointing out that Myrtle never really worried if Miles's lights were on in the house or not.

She said, "Well, come on in! Let's have a snack." Myrtle was pleased as punch that Miles was there. She'd never actually entertained Miles during a middle-of-the-night visit and now she felt almost as if she were hosting a party. Myrtle pulled out an old cheese tray that she'd had since the 1950s. It had a dark wooden back encasing a circular ceramic plate with large yellow daisies on it. She found a block of cheese in her fridge and some crackers in the pantry. For good measure, she also placed a few chocolate cookies on the cheese tray and filled up two glasses with milk.

Miles had already sat down at the kitchen table. "No," said Myrtle, "let's go sit in the living room like grown-ups. We'll be more comfortable in there anyway."

Miles helped her carry everything into the living room and they put the food and drinks on the coffee table, pushing aside some books to make room. Myrtle gave a satisfied sigh. "All right then. Oh! The napkins." And she was off again.

When everything was finally set, she said, "Now, tell me why you couldn't sleep, Miles."

He blinked at her and didn't answer until he'd carefully finished swallowing the bit of cookie he was eating. "That's what you want to know? I thought you'd want to talk about what you found out yesterday at Felix's office and bounce some ideas off me."

Myrtle said, "No, I really want to know why you can't sleep." She leaned forward expectantly.

Miles seemed pleased by this. "Well, at first I thought it was because I had something of an upset stomach. But then I realized that I had something on my mind that was keeping me from sleeping."

"Was it something to do with Cosette's drop-in?" asked Myrtle.

"No. It was something to do with Tobin. Actually, it had to do with Tobin's attire."

Myrtle frowned. She had to admit that Tobin's clothing hadn't made that much of an impression on her, one way or another. "Wasn't he wearing work clothes? Jeans and a tee shirt is what I remember."

Miles pushed his rimless glasses up his nose. "He was. But I realized tonight how very *clean* those clothes were. His white tee shirt was completely white, and there was no dirt or dust on his jeans. His boots even looked clean. I know when I do any kind of yard work, I end up covered with clods of dry grass or weeds or dirt."

Myrtle frowned. "I hadn't thought about it, but you're right, Miles. So what does that mean? Had he already completed the yard work and gone home to change and then return to the cemetery? Or had he not even started the work yet? I guess the most important thing the answer to those questions would indicate is the time of death. If we know the time of death, then it's going to help us eliminate suspects. Especially since Red isn't good about sharing important details like time of death with me." Myrtle made a face. "But didn't Joan say that she saw Tobin alive and well when she was dropping Noah off at Elaine's house? She saw him doing yard work there at ten o'clock."

"What if Joan is lying?" asked Miles.

Myrtle nodded. "Right. If she's lying, then she really doesn't have an alibi for the time of the murder. She says that after she arrived at Elaine's house, she visited for a while and then went right to the funeral. So she's got Elaine for an alibi. But if Tobin were already *dead*, then she doesn't."

"Although it somehow seems unlikely to me that Joan would have stopped on the way to her babysitter's house, whacked Tobin over the head with his own shovel while Noah waited in the car, and then toddled over to Elaine's house as if nothing happened." Miles took a sip of milk and then carefully dabbed at his mouth with a napkin.

"No, that's *precisely* the way to commit murder," said Myrtle. "Who's going to suspect the mommy in the minivan?" She nodded. "So that's why you haven't gotten any sleep tonight. Tobin's clothes."

"Did you find out anything yesterday?" asked Miles curiously. "Wasn't it Felix that you'd been planning to talk with?"

"It was. Although Felix wasn't especially helpful. Guess who was way more helpful than Felix?"

"Who?"

"Puddin," said Myrtle. She balanced a piece of cheese on a soda cracker and popped it into her mouth.

"Puddin?" Miles sat back in surprise. He glanced around the living room, his eye skimming over the mantel over the stone fireplace, the dark wood of various tables, and pausing over the coffee table in front of them. "You mean Puddin cleaned here recently?"

Myrtle made a face. "Yes, I know. Dust is everywhere. But you know how Puddin is."

"I sure do. How on earth could she possibly be helpful with information when she's not even helpful doing the job you're paying her to do?" asked Miles.

"She's extremely good at gossiping and avoiding work. Puddin is also surprisingly well connected in the housekeeping underworld. She told me that Sybil is practically stalking Felix, who's really not all that interested in her."

"Is that so?" Miles blinked in surprise. "Sybil actually isn't a bad-looking woman, by any stretch."

"Spoken like a man," said Myrtle in exasperation. "The problem is more that she doesn't seem to have a glimmer of an intelligent thought in that attractive head of hers. She is a pleasant space cadet."

"So what's Sybil's motive again?" asked Miles.

"She wants to eliminate a potential rival for her affections," said Myrtle with some asperity. Really, Miles must still be half-asleep. He wasn't connecting the dots at all.

"*Tobin*?"

"Not Tobin! Sybil was worried that *Cosette* was stealing Felix's heart." Myrtle saw Miles trying to swallow a smile and rolled her eyes. "You were kidding."

"I was, sorry. But seriously, going back to Tobin's murder. Why would Sybil murder Tobin?" Miles looked at the cookies, looked away, hesitated, and then decided to take another one. Myrtle thought that made five cookies for Miles. Good luck getting to sleep after that much sugar.

"Same reason why anyone else would kill Tobin. While he was dumping that bag of garbage on Cosette's front porch, he clearly saw something. Maybe he saw someone sneaking from around the back of the house. Maybe he saw someone there who had claimed that they *weren't* there that night. The murderer wanted to make sure he didn't have the chance to tell anyone what he saw," said Myrtle.

Miles nodded and picked up his glass. "So the Felix visit was a bust, huh? Did you at least end up with a life insurance policy?" His eyes were merry over the rim of his glass.

"Just about! I told him I'd have to carefully consider spending that kind of money. I have a feeling that Felix is going to keep after me, now that he thinks I'm a genuine lead. He's going to guilt me into getting a plan to provide for those dreaded "final expenses." Myrtle stared glumly down at her empty plate.

Miles choked on his milk and it took him a moment to recover. "Final expenses. Wow! That must have been a cheerful meeting. Especially since, knowing you, you've got your final expenses all prepared and paid for anyway."

"Exactly. And a meager amount it took, too! Yes, a very cheerful meeting between Felix and me." Myrtle made a face.

"Were you able to get back on the more cheerful subject of murder?"

"Sort of. He denies all. He acted as if he weren't even at Cosette's party—until I told him I'd seen him there. Then he immediately started minimizing his brief appearance at the drop-in," said Myrtle.

"How could he minimize an argument that we witnessed?" asked Miles, tilting his head to one side. "We could tell Felix was angry, even if we didn't understand what he was so upset over. Sybil was clearly the most upset, but Felix was smoldering. And Cosette looked as if she were part of the argument, too."

"Oh, it *wasn't* an argument, you see, Miles. It was a political discussion. About Congress." Myrtle rolled her eyes. "I do hate it when people treat the elderly as if they're children. Felix was completely underestimating me."

"Which probably moves him to the top of the suspect list," said Miles with a grin.

"Probably."

There was a knock at the front door and Miles and Myrtle stared at each other in surprise. "Am I having a party?" asked Myrtle. "What a pity we ate all the food."

She ambled to the front door, clutching her cane. Myrtle was assuming that she was going to see Red's face when she looked through the front window, and she did. He had his police uniform on.

"Is it Red?" asked Miles. "I don't think we're being noisy enough for Erma to come over and tell us to hold it down."

"Heaven forbid," said Myrtle. "Yes, it's Red." She turned and grinned at Miles. "Should I let him in?"

Red knocked a bit more impatiently at the door and Myrtle sighed and unlocked it.

"Mama, for a minute I thought you weren't going to let me in," he said. He glanced over at Miles, sitting there in his plaid pajamas and bathrobe without any sign of surprise. "Hi there, Miles. Y'all having an Insomniacs Anonymous meeting again?"

"Apparently, you need to join the group," said Myrtle sourly. "What are you doing in your uniform?"

"Well Mama, I'm headed off to work. It's almost five o'clock now. Some folks are getting up and starting their day."

"You're not usually up this early to go to the police station, are you?" Myrtle lifted her eyebrows with surprise.

"I am when there are a couple of unsolved murders on my watch, that's for sure. The SBI expects it."

Myrtle knew the SBI was the North Carolina state police. "Is that nice Detective Lieutenant Perkins helping you out again?"

"He is. Although he's probably wondering what's wrong with our tiny town to make it have such a high murder rate," said Red, plopping down in one of Myrtle's armchairs.

"Small towns brew up strong feelings," said Myrtle. "You know that." She sat back down in her chair. "So what brings you by? Did you want a snack before you go to the station?"

"I remembered I never did get a statement from you at the funeral, although I was with you part of the time in question," said Red. He sighed. "It would be nice if you stopped discovering bodies. It looks suspicious." He took a small notebook and pencil out of the front pocket of his uniform and waited expectantly.

"Well, there's not a whole lot to say," said Myrtle. "Miles and I arrived late to the funeral, as you know."

"Flat tire," interjected Miles, for the record.

"Yes. Anyway, I saw what appeared to be a body some yards away in the woods. I mentioned that fact to you," she said, arching her eyebrows at her son. "You ignored me. I investigated further. It was Tobin. He was dead." She shrugged. "End of story."

He sighed. "Mama, the reason I ignored you is because it was highly unlikely that there was going to be another body. Especially in the cemetery."

"I'd think the cemetery was the perfect place for bodies," said Myrtle.

"Non-buried bodies. You know what I mean," said Red, rolling his eyes.

"Considering the number of bodies racking up in Bradley, I'd say there was a fairly high likelihood that I was correct."

Red pressed his lips together, and then asked, "Did you see Tobin earlier that day?"

"No."

Miles glanced at Myrtle to see if she was going to elaborate on that, but she didn't. Miles cleared his throat. "Red, are y'all thinking that Tobin died first thing in the morning or shortly before the funeral?"

Red gave him a regretful look. "I'd like to be able to answer that, Miles, but we're trying to keep the details of the case under wraps."

"Surely you can at least confirm that Tobin was murdered with a shovel," said Myrtle. "Considering that the shovel was right there next to him and I didn't notice that Tobin's body was riddled with bullets or anything."

Red hesitated. "Yes, I guess that's okay. I can confirm that it was blunt force trauma resulting from a blow from the nearby shovel. And you know that information doesn't need to go right into the *Bradley Bugle*." He frowned. "Oh, never mind, I just remembered that the new reporter is covering this story. At least, that's what Sloan was saying."

"Sloan has absolutely no clue," said Myrtle with a sniff. "I'll have a lot more juicy tidbits than that Tina will."

"Kim," said Miles.

"Whatever."

"By the way, I thought that Friday the Thirteenth tip column you did was fantastic," said Red, a gleam of genuine admiration in his eyes. "You've still 'got it', Mama. People have been telling me how much they enjoyed that article."

Myrtle glared down at her empty plate. Great. A moment of genius that happened completely by accident.

As soon as Red and Miles left, Myrtle sat down at her computer and feverishly started writing a news story.

Chapter Thirteen

Myrtle slept in later than she'd planned that morning. Considering that she didn't turn in until six a.m., she didn't feel too scandalized that she'd awakened at ten-thirty in the morning. What *did* scandalize her was the fact that her doorbell was ringing.

She muttered a couple of choice words for the doorbell, pulled on a bathrobe (inside-out, as she unhappily discovered later), and patted at her white hair, which was standing up like Einstein's again. Myrtle staggered to the front door since she couldn't figure out in her sleepy stupor where her cane was.

She peered apprehensively through the front window, saw Wanda, the psychic, and instantly relaxed. Wanda, or *Wander*, as her brother called her, lived off the old highway in a shack covered with hubcaps. The rotting sign on the highway advertised Wanda's services as: *Madam Zora, sykick*. No dressing up was needed. But Myrtle did feel a slight frisson of unease. Wanda, as much as Myrtle might pooh-pooh it, did seem to have some sort of gift, although she was rather too fond of giving Myrtle dire prophesies.

Wanda looked steadily at her as she opened the door. "Rough night?" she grated in her cigarette-ruined voice.

"I guess you could say that. A sleepless one, anyway. Come on in," said Myrtle, opening her door wide.

Wanda was stick-thin with nicotine-stained hands. She was missing quite a few teeth, and wore nondescript clothing that hung on her bony frame.

"Breakfast?" asked Myrtle, thinking that Wanda looked like she could use a good few meals. "Let's see. I have lots of cereal. Unless you want eggs, bacon, and toast?"

There apparently was no question which Wanda would want. Myrtle quickly found herself breaking open some eggs and sticking slices of toast in the toaster.

"How did you get here, anyway?" asked Myrtle. "I didn't notice a car out front."

"The cars is broke," said Wanda with a shrug of a skeletal shoulder.

"All of them? The cars in your yard aren't working?" Myrtle turned away from the stove to look at Wanda in surprise. "Why, your yard is filled to bursting with cars."

"Them? They's up on cement blocks. Broke."

"Oh." Myrtle did recall that there seemed to be a lot of cement blocks in the yard. She pushed the eggs around in the skillet. "So how *did* you get here?"

"Walked," said Wanda calmly.

Myrtle stared at her. "Walked? From the old highway? That must have taken you hours! Can't you pick up the phone to call?"

"Phone is broke," said Wanda with another shrug. She raised a painted-on eyebrow. "Eggs need movin'."

Myrtle jumped and quickly started scrambling the eggs again. Then, deciding they were done, she scooped them off onto plates, added a couple of pieces of microwaved bacon, and quickly buttered up some toast. She poured them both some milk, then sat down with Wanda at her kitchen table.

Wanda made short work of the breakfast and Myrtle watched it quickly disappear, deciding not to question why she was here until Wanda had finished eating. In fact, Wanda finished so quickly that she never even got a chance to ask her a thing—Myrtle was still working on a slice of bacon.

"Guess you was wantin' to know why I'm here," said Wanda, shifting in her seat. Myrtle guessed that she wanted to have a cigarette and was relieved that she didn't seem to have any with her.

Myrtle nodded. "Although I believe I know why." She steeled herself. Wanda always provided her with dire predictions.

"You're in danger," said Wanda, looking at Myrtle steadily.

Myrtle jumped a bit as Pasha leapt through her cracked kitchen window and bolted over to Wanda. The cat launched itself into Wanda's lap. Myrtle opened her mouth to apologize, and then shut it again, noticing that Wanda was languidly stroking the feral cat, cool as a cucumber.

"How did I know you were going to say that I'm in danger?" asked Myrtle, after taking a sip of her milk. "You never give me any happy predictions, Wanda. It's never 'you'll go on a trip to foreign lands' or 'a mysterious man will come into your life and make you happy.' No, it's always 'your life is in danger.' You're like a broken record."

Wanda shrugged. "And *you* are always in danger." She petted Pasha, who was purring loudly.

"We're a pair then," said Myrtle. She waited for more information from Wanda, but the woman was already gently setting Pasha on the floor, standing up, and heading for the door. "Hold on a minute. Don't you have more information than that? Did your crystal ball suddenly fog up?"

Wanda gave her a disdainful look. "Wasn't the ball. Was the cards."

"The tarot cards? Didn't they at least indicate where this danger was coming from? Am I going to be stricken with the flu? Will I unknowingly tread into an open manhole while strolling to the store? Is a desperate killer going to cut my life short?" Myrtle threw up her hands in frustration. "That message is absolutely no good to me. I need more information."

Wanda stared at her coolly. "The cards said you…should take up knitting."

Myrtle gaped at her, then glanced around her room for signs of knitting paraphernalia—there were none. “I don’t suppose Red or Elaine paid you to say that, did they?”

Wanda gave her a puzzled look.

“Great,” said Myrtle under her breath. “Here, wait. Where are you going?”

“Time to go home,” said Wanda. She walked out the door.

“I can’t let you walk an hour home,” said Myrtle. “I’ll drive you back.”

The psychic raised an eyebrow and glanced at Myrtle’s carless driveway.

“I don’t drive anymore,” said Myrtle with a sigh. “That is, I *do* drive and I actually have a license that doesn’t have to be renewed for the next fifteen years.” She glanced over to see if the psychic was impressed by that, but she didn’t seem to be. Myrtle continued, “I don’t have a car anymore. Red convinced me that it’s better for me to get exercise and that I was never really going very far anyway and could use the money from the sale of the car. But I’m sure it was to discourage me from driving.”

“Does it?” asked Wanda.

“Sometimes it does discourage me. Sometimes, I’ll borrow someone else’s car if I feel like going for a drive. Like your cousin Miles’s.” Myrtle successfully squashed the chuckle that threatened to spill out. The thought of the oh-so-correct Miles and Wanda being related always amused Myrtle. They had recently, to Miles’s utter dismay, discovered the familial connection.

Miles wasn’t excited to see either Myrtle or Wanda at his front door. He was dressed, but appeared very sleepy. “You want to borrow my car?” He squinted doubtfully at Myrtle. “I don’t know. It never seems to work out very well when you borrow it. I'll drive you." He turned around to head back inside. "Let me get my keys."

"In your pocket," said Wanda, sounding bored. It must get tiring to always know everything, thought Myrtle.

"Right." Miles gave Wanda a sharp look. "All right then. Let's head on out."

Miles was apparently in somewhat of a hurry. Myrtle clutched the car door as they flew down the road to Wanda's house. She'd nodded her thanks, given Myrtle a stern look as if reminding her that she needed to watch her step, and disappeared into the hubcap-covered shack.

Miles gave a relieved sigh. "Well, that's done. What was she doing hanging out at your house, anyway?"

"Oh, you know. She had to issue me a harrowing prophecy," said Myrtle with a shrug. "I'm in danger, yada-yada-yada. And I think that Red and Elaine must have paid her to tell me to take up knitting. It was most bizarre how she brought that up."

Miles still had a distasteful expression on his face, just thinking about Wanda.

"I can't think why you have such an objection to poor Wanda. Especially since she's family," added Myrtle a bit slyly.

Miles shifted uncomfortably. "I suppose because of that family connection. And maybe because I think I should be doing more for her."

"Don't forget her brother," said Myrtle in an innocent voice. "There's Crazy Dan, too."

Miles appeared to be suffering some indigestion, according to his coloring. "Yes. I'm sort of horrified by them, but feel somewhat guilty also."

"They don't seem to want anything from you or anyone else, Miles. They read a few fortunes and sell a couple of hubcaps or maybe some peanuts or live bait, and they make a living. Not what you and I would call a *good* living, but a living all the same."

That apparently cheered Miles up a bit and he looked less anxious as they headed back toward Bradley.

Myrtle figured she might as well take advantage of his better mood. "Do you mind running me by the library on the way back? I was going to get those book club books we were talking about and head over to Sybil's house."

"You don't need me to go with you to Sybil's, do you?" Miles looked alarmed.

"Why? Worried that Sybil will switch allegiance and start stalking you instead?"

"I hardly think that I make an appropriate target for her," said Miles stiffly. "I'm old enough to be her father. And retired. There's nothing very glamorous about me."

"There's nothing very glamorous about Felix either. He's all business. I can't think what Sybil sees in him," said Myrtle. "I guess everyone's different."

"So—do you need me to take you there, then?" asked Miles.

"No. It's only a short walk from the library to Sybil's house. And I'm only going to be carrying a couple of books and my cane."

"How will you manage that?" Miles frowned.

Myrtle reached into her purse and pulled out a compact tote bag. "By being prepared," she said with a grin.

Chapter Fourteen

Myrtle glanced over the neat rows of books. She decided to bring over a couple of choices—a book she would actually *like* to have the book club read, and a book that Sybil would most likely want the book club to read. This would have the added benefit of not only giving her the opportunity to quiz Sybil on the murders, but also possibly even giving her the chance to pitch *real* literature at their book club.

Thinking about book club made Myrtle grouchy, so she tried to refocus on the rows of books. She found an old favorite, Eudora Welty's *The Optimist's Daughter*, and pulled it gingerly from the stacks. Myrtle placed it carefully in her tote bag and then looked back at the shelves with a critical frown.

There was a novel written by a celebrity that looked absolutely atrocious, but Myrtle didn't want anyone to think she even knew who this celebrity was. There was a book featuring a beach and a middle-aged woman staring thoughtfully off into the sunset. Myrtle made a face. That accurately depicted eighty-percent of the books that the book club had chosen over the past eighteen months. She shouldn't take this one over to Sybil's because it might be one of the books she was supposed to have read for the club and hadn't.

Then Myrtle spotted it. *Life Is a Soap Opera*. She opened the book and saw some similarity between her favorite soap, *Tomorrow's Promise*, and some woman experiencing midlife crisis. Perfect. She chucked it into her tote bag and fished her library card out of her pocketbook.

Myrtle raised her eyebrows when she saw who was standing in the checkout line in front of her: Joan. She had a stack of children's picture books that the librarian was quickly checking out. Noah stood next to her and he turned and smiled at Myrtle in recognition. "Mama," he said, pulling at Joan's pants leg.

Joan took the books and turned around. "Hi, Miss Myrtle!"

"Well, hi there! Did you find some good books, Noah?"

Noah nodded and pointed to one of the books that Joan was holding. "I've got one with a dump truck!"

A closer look at the stack of books showed not a single one was on the subject of biochemistry or calculus. Clearly, it must have been Cosette pushing Noah to learn foreign languages and pursue academics. Joan and Noah had picked out books about trucks, construction, dinosaurs, and fairy tales. It sure seemed more appropriate for a preschooler.

Joan's mind appeared to be running on the same track as she looked down at the books she was carrying. "You know, my mother is probably rolling in her grave that I'm checking these out." She put a hand over her mouth as if regretting what she'd said, but she didn't seem that regretful. "It's just that Mother was always pushing Noah to read these super-academic books when all he really wanted to do was see pictures of front-loader trucks and bulldozers."

Myrtle nodded. "Oh, I know. When Red was a little guy, sometimes we'd walk over to watch construction sites. He'd be entertained for hours."

Joan snapped her fingers. "This is off the subject, but I just remembered that I need to get that container back to you—the one the soup came in." For some reason, Joan didn't seem to want to meet Myrtle's eyes now. Had something happened to the container?

"No hurry, my dear. Whenever you think of it." Except that she really did want another chance to talk to Joan about the case later on. "Although—well, I do tend to use that container myself quite a bit."

"I'll bring it by tomorrow or the next day," said Joan. "No worries."

"I was wondering," said Myrtle innocently. "You had mentioned seeing poor Tobin the morning he died…that he was already working in the cemetery when you were driving Noah over to Elaine's house. Are you quite sure that you saw *Tobin* then? And that he was doing yard work?"

Joan's face flushed and she glanced away at Noah, who was tugging on her pant leg again. "Noah, wait." She took a deep breath and turned back to Myrtle, saying brightly, "I sure did. I was thinking that it was a good thing that he'd gotten such an early start, since it was rapidly becoming such a hot day. He was working hard." She sighed as Noah starting pulling at her again. "Nice talking to you, Miss Myrtle. I guess I'll have to be going now."

Myrtle watched absently as the librarian checked out her books. Interesting that Joan was so insistent that she'd seen Tobin working hard in the cemetery…when he didn't have any dirt, stains, or sweat on his clothing. Could she be covering up for someone? Herself?

Sybil didn't live far from the library. Myrtle had been there for book club once and remembered it as a small, untidy home nearly overrun by tchotchkes. Sybil had apparently either visited or lived in a variety of places, judging from the Mardi Gras beads, souvenir thimbles, and other knickknacks. Sybil hadn't been expecting her, so she wasn't her usual, carefully made-up self. In many ways, she seemed prettier—certainly younger—without all the makeup she usually glopped on. She still wore a peasant dress and huge hoop earrings, though.

To her credit, if she were annoyed by a sudden visit from an elderly lady bearing books, she certainly showed absolutely no sign of it. "Look at you! Walking all this way to talk to me about books! Come on in and let's have a nice visit."

Myrtle was immediately relieved of her tote bag and hustled into the crowded living room.

"I'll get us some soft drinks. Or tea? Which do you want?"

"Tea would be lovely, if you've got it." Myrtle reminded herself she needed to play up the doddering old lady if she was going to pull this visit off.

While Sybil was getting their drinks, Myrtle looked around with wide eyes. She'd been worried about staring during the book club, but now had the opportunity to take in all the Russian nesting dolls (with politicians' faces on them), ceramic cats, plastic candy dispensers made to look like cartoon characters, snow globes, and kewpie dolls. It was completely overwhelming.

Well, if she couldn't say anything nice, she wouldn't say anything at all. Her expression would surely give her away if she tried to give a false compliment. She entertained herself by taking the books out of the tote bag that Sybil had put at her feet.

Then she had a sudden thought. If Sybil were so besotted with Felix (and he was so compulsively neat that Myrtle couldn't even imagine him being in this room), then wouldn't there be evidence of that in the room somewhere? Sybil had placed her on a sofa where she had a clearer view of the built-in shelves of her various collectables, so Myrtle craned her neck to look around. Then she spotted, behind her on a sofa table, a long row of framed photos of Felix. Felix alone, Felix looking solemn with a laughing Sybil, Felix ignoring the camera—possibly not even aware that Sybil was around.

"Here we are!" sang out Sybil, bringing in a small tray of drinks. The tray was wildly colorful and looked as if it might have originally hailed from an island souvenir shop.

"By the way, Miss Myrtle, I've been wanting to tell you for a while how much I admire your darling gnome collection. It's precious, truly precious, and I've been longing to congratulate you on it. It must really have taken you a while to collect them all."

It stung just a bit that Sybil admired her gnomes. "Why, thanks," said Myrtle. "It has taken me much of the last thirty-five years or so. I started collecting them when Red was a teenager and he did things to drive me crazy. He sure hated it when I put the gnomes in the front yard, so it became the perfect way of getting back at him for being disrespectful or moody, or whatever."

She hesitated because Sybil was now looking at her expectantly. Oh. Apparently, she needed to admire all the knickknacks. "And you have some…amazing…collections here." Amazing was a word that she could use completely genuinely, so she felt proud of herself. "You must have a lot of fun with them."

"I sure do," Sybil beamed as she glanced across at her treasures. Then her expression darkened as she stared at something behind Myrtle's head. The photos of Felix. Sybil jerked her gaze away from the photos and gave Myrtle an awkward smile. "So, you're here for a reason, I'm sure, although it's nice to see you, no matter what."

Sybil seemed so sweet that Myrtle really hated thinking that she was probably a two-time murderer and a stalker. Really, she did. But she sensed that underneath that sweetness was some weirdness, too.

"Yes, and I do hope this is a good time," said Myrtle in the fluffy old lady voice that she trotted out from time to time. "You see, it's my month to pick the book club book and I wanted some advice. You always do such a good job picking them." Myrtle had to swallow hard here when bile rose in her throat for saying such a falsehood.

Sybil blinked at her with her long eyelashes. "Do I? You know, I thought somebody at book club told me that you weren't all that wild about my book picks."

Myrtle gave a gale of nervous laughter. "Ha-ha! Did they? Such jokers in our club. But good friends aren't they?"

"They have been. Of course, I'm trying to get used to living in Bradley still. The ladies have been really welcoming. Well, most of them." Sybil made a face. "Let's see those books you've brought over."

"All right." Myrtle pulled out the Eudora Welty book and held it out to Sybil. "This is one of my favorites, actually. I thought it might appeal to a group of Southern ladies."

"And Miles," added Sybil with a laugh. "He's the rooster in the hen house, isn't he?"

"He wouldn't miss a single meeting either," said Myrtle, rolling her eyes. "He secretly revels in being the center of attention at book club, I think."

Sybil was slowly flipping through the book and Myrtle could tell that the fact it was a piece of genuine literature made it completely unappealing to her. "I'm sure this is a great book, Miss Myrtle. For book club, though? I just don't know. It looks really old."

"Old? It was one of Welty's later works. In 1972."

Sybil gave her a wry look. "Miss Myrtle, 1972 was a long time ago."

Myrtle snorted. "It was only yesterday, Sybil. When you have a few more years on you, then you'll have more of a real perspective on time."

She realized that she was possibly caring too much about the book club selection. Particularly since this was focusing merely as a trumped-up reason to interview Sybil about the murders. But she couldn't seem to help herself—this was a topic that was near and dear to her heart. "You see," continued Myrtle eagerly, "I've been thinking for a while that we might upgrade our selection of books. You know—stretch ourselves. Expand our minds. Go on armchair adventures with fictional companions who actually make for good company."

Sybil's gaze was a bit glazed-over. "Books are for relaxing, Miss Myrtle. Life is too hard to have reading be tough, too." She closed *The Optimist's Daughter*. "What was the other book you brought?"

Myrtle felt a tremendous reluctance to hand over the other book, then told herself to snap out of it. She couldn't somehow have really thought she would change Sybil's mind about the direction of book club, could she? For heaven's sake—it wasn't even really her month to choose the book. She handed over the other book. "This one seemed more in keeping with the kind of thing we've been reading in the club."

Sybil's face lit up when she saw the title. "Oh, I've heard of this one. It's supposed to be so funny. And true—life *can* be a soap opera, can't it?" The dark shadows ran across her face again.

Since influencing a change of book club direction seemed completely impossible, Myrtle returned to the real reason for her visit. But she couldn't scare Sybil off or she really wouldn't get anything out of coming here.

"Have you had some troubles, dear? You looked so distressed there, for a second." Myrtle gave her what she hoped was an innocently concerned look.

Sybil patted the pockets of her exercise clothing, apparently for a non-existent tissue. Myrtle promptly pulled one from a packet in her huge pocketbook and held it out to her.

Sybil blew her nose emphatically. "Miss Myrtle, I'm in a love affair with someone very special to me. We're absolutely perfect together in every way—he's the man I've been dreaming of for all these years."

"Does he not share your feelings?" asked Myrtle sympathetically.

"That's the thing. He *does*. He's absolutely, completely, overwhelmingly in love. But he's a very business-oriented man and doesn't recognize that emotion when he sees it," said Sybil.

This sounded like an opinion that Sybil had repeated to herself over and over again until she believed it to be true.

"Have you been a couple long?" asked Myrtle.

Sybil looked impatient—whether with Myrtle or Felix, Myrtle couldn't tell. "We've been soul mates for forever. Felix has had a hard time adjusting, that's all. Plus, that woman was getting in the way."

Myrtle gave her a guileless look. "A woman?"

"You know. That Cosette Whitlow. Felix kept fancying himself in love with her." Sybil gave a barking laugh meant to spotlight the ridiculousness of that belief.

"I thought I might have spotted the two of you at Cosette's drop-in," said Myrtle in a mild tone. "Everyone looked unhappy. Were you arguing?"

Sybil rubbed her eyes. "What a night. Felix kept saying he wanted to go to Cosette's party. He was being real ornery about it. And I knew that Cosette was a huge flirt who seemed to think she was a lot prettier than she really was. I told Felix I didn't want to go over there and have Cosette flirt the whole time and he said that he was going to go whether I wanted to or not."

"But it seemed to me," said Myrtle carefully, "that Felix was angry with Cosette. It seemed like he was warning her in some way."

Sybil shook a finger at her. "Exactly. Bingo. I think Cosette was acting too flirty with Felix in public and he was telling her to back off. But I didn't hear that part because I walked into the kitchen too late—remember when I left you and Miles to go into the kitchen?" She gave a harsh laugh. "If he'd only listened to me. I could have told him that Cosette was no good for him."

So there hadn't been any political argument. Felix had been breaking up with Cosette...as he was trying rather unsuccessfully to do with Sybil. Just as she'd suspected.

"So you think Cosette was being too edgy with their relationship?" asked Myrtle.

"I bet it's because she wouldn't leave him alone and he didn't want a scandal," said Sybil. She shrugged. "A professional guy like him doesn't want to be seen around with a married woman. He's supposed to be building up trust with clients. Besides," she said, holding out her hands, "he and I are a couple. So it made sense that he would try to make her see that."

"Wasn't that such a horrible night?" asked Myrtle in her best gossipy voice, trying to set the stage for her next questions. "I guess you must have heard that I discovered Cosette in the back yard."

Sybil raised her eyebrows. "No, I sure didn't. I figured that Felix had looked for her and found her." She leaned forward and gave Myrtle a sympathetic squeeze on the hand. "That must have been horrible for you."

"It was. And it's dreadful that the murderer is still at large. Poor Red, working so hard to try to find out who did it. *You* didn't happen to see or hear anything when you were leaving the party with Felix, did you?"

Sybil studied her ceiling as she thought. "Let's see. Nope." She looked back at Myrtle with a regretful smile. "I was in such a tizzy with Felix being mad that I don't even remember our drive back home. I told Red the same thing. I was as good as useless that night."

"You didn't happen to see," said Myrtle slowly, "a man carrying garbage *toward* the house instead of away from it?"

Sybil looked startled. "As a matter of fact, I saw a man carrying trash across the street, apparently on his way to the Whitlow house. Weird. I'd forgotten about it, too."

Maybe it jogged her memory in other ways, too.

"So you saw a man with trash. Did you notice anything else? You must have felt awkward, leaving the drop-in with Felix looking so angry. Did you look around you to see who else was at their cars, who might be watching as y'all made a scene?" asked Myrtle.

Now Sybil appeared to be thinking about it in earnest. "Erma Sherman was outside—from book club, you know."

"I know," said Myrtle with a sigh. "She's my next-door neighbor."

"Poor you," said Sybil. "Anyway, I winced when I saw her because I knew that she loves to gossip; and there was Felix, practically pulling me away from the party and looking mad enough to pop." She thought some more. "There were some people I didn't know who were leaving or coming. I didn't worry about them, since I didn't know them and Felix apparently didn't, either." She paused. "And I saw Joan—Cosette and Lucas's daughter."

Myrtle said, "Joan? You saw her leaving?" But Joan should already have left by that point.

"No, I saw her pulling in. She was looking for a spot to park and ended up parking way down the street instead of trying to parallel park closer. I remember thinking that she was super-late to the drop-in, even though drop-ins are more laid back, and wondered where her son was…because when she got out of the car, she didn't have him with her. She started walking around the side of the house, which was weird."

Myrtle waited for a few moments to see if Sybil was able to come up with anything else, but she shook her head. "That's it, I think."

Myrtle said, "Isn't it amazing how things come back to us? I don't suppose you remember anything about the day of that other murder—Tobin Tinker's."

Sybil shook her head once again. "No, I'm sure I won't be able to help you there. I have no idea who Tobin is. I guess in a lot of ways I'm still a newcomer to Bradley since I don't know everyone in town, like most folks do."

"Tobin is actually the man you saw carrying the trash toward the party," said Myrtle quietly.

Sybil gasped. "Oh no. Really? That's such a coincidence."

"Is it? I believe the police think the two murders are connected. How could they not be?" asked Myrtle. "Did you happen to notice anything at Cosette's funeral that might give us some clues what happened to Tobin?"

Sybil shook her head and looked away. "I didn't go to Cosette's funeral, Miss Myrtle. Funerals are for paying respects. If you don't have any respect, you don't go."

Myrtle stared intently at Sybil until she looked at her. "I saw you there, though. I saw you by the road. Maybe you didn't listen to the service or stand with the mourners, but you were watching from a distance. Your car really stands out, you know. Did you see anything while you were there?"

Sybil seemed to be about to protest again that she hadn't been there, and then she shrugged. She rattled the ice in her glass. "I wasn't there because there was a funeral. I was trying to figure out what was going on near the woods. I could tell people were grouped funny for a funeral—for one thing, they weren't standing near the grave or around Lucas, like you'd expect. For another, they all looked shocked. Funerals can be sad, but they're usually not shocking to go to."

Myrtle nodded. "And you found out later that there was a body in the woods. When you heard that, did you think of anything you saw when you were down by the road?"

"I didn't see a thing," said Sybil. "Not a thing. Now tell me more about where you got your gnomes. Have you ever ordered any online?"

Chapter Fifteen

As Myrtle was walking back home, she decided she wanted her container back from Lucas. She hadn't spoken to him as much as she'd talked with the other suspects. And, pitiful though he was, he certainly *was* a suspect. He was the husband and he was getting, according to his daughter, a tidy windfall from the life insurance company. Hazel and Joan had both mentioned the fact that he'd been broke before Cosette died. He was decidedly grief-stricken, but maybe he was only grief-stricken over the state of his soul.

The books, neither of which she had the smallest intention of introducing to the book club—especially since it wasn't actually her turn for six months—were starting to weigh heavily on her as she walked. Myrtle decided that she'd go by the library to return them before walking to Lucas's house.

The library was a two-story brick building with a few too many steps for Myrtle's liking. She stood at the bottom of the flight of stone stairs and sighed. This one time, she'd use the ramp on the side of the stairs. She'd used the stairs earlier, after all. No one would ever know.

She mentally cursed the humidity of Southern summers for the millionth time as she walked up the steep ramp. The glassed-in foyer was blessedly air-conditioned and she hovered in there a few minutes after sticking the two books in the return slot. After she felt more or less refreshed, she turned to go back out and down the ramp again.

It had been very quiet on the street. It must be considered too hot for folks to walk around town, which Myrtle hadn't gotten the memo on. Going down the handicapped ramp was more challenging than going up, although surely that shouldn't be the case, since it required less exertion.

She'd just put one foot down on the ramp in front of her when she felt a sudden prickling at the back of her neck and a sense of movement behind her. A hand briefly and firmly pressed to the base of her back and shoved hard. Myrtle started falling as she heard the sound of someone running away.

It was her cane—that hated cane— that saved her in the end. Her feet had swung out in front of her and her hand had flown off the rail from the force of her fall. But somehow she'd automatically tightened her grip on her cane with that left hand and jammed down the stick as if she were skiing. It helped her to sit down, albeit very hard, on the concrete ramp. That's where she sat, trembling and motionless, until a car drove up to park in front of the library.

When she looked up, she was appalled to see that it was a police car and that Red was hurrying out. Shoot. What was he going to think?

Red quickly indicated what he was thinking. "You fell! Mama, are you okay?"

Myrtle wasn't sure if she was okay, but she didn't think anything had broken. And she certainly wasn't going to own this accident as a fall. She gingerly started moving her arms and legs. "I'm okay. But I didn't fall, I was pushed."

Red's face went from relief that she wasn't hurt to skepticism. "Right. You never fall down, do you?"

"Red, I was *shoved.* I returned a couple of books and I was cautiously making my way down the ramp, and someone came up and pushed me! Look around the library and see if there are any suspects lurking around in there."

Red said, "Suspects? Mama, I'm more interested in getting you off the staircase and over to a doctor to make sure you're all right."

Myrtle bristled. "I'm fine. I sure don't need a doctor's co-pay on top of everything else. This spill will only mean a few bruises. And if you won't scour the library for who might be responsible, then I guess I'll have to do it." She struggled to get to her feet, feeling the beginnings of bruising and soreness. Red supported her by her elbows and helped bring her up.

"Let me help you into the library and out of the heat, Mama. I think the heat might be addling your mind a bit—you're making less sense than usual." He gently took her arm and led her into the library. Myrtle found that she was leaning more on both her cane and Red's arm than she wanted to. She could also tell that she was going to be very, very sore.

Red led her over to the first available armchair and helped her into it. She ended up dropping down as her legs plumb gave way. Red stared solicitously at her and Myrtle frowned back at him. "Don't worry about me. Go check out the patrons, for heaven's sake." She looked fretfully around her, but didn't see anyone but Gladys, the librarian, who was hurrying toward them with furrowed brows and an anxious look in her eyes. She'd been the Bradley librarian since Myrtle had gotten her first library card. Myrtle knew how old that must make Gladys. It irritated Myrtle that Gladys didn't appear that old. And that *she* wasn't the one who was wondering how she was going to make it back out of this chair.

"I'm fine, I'm fine," muttered Myrtle.

Gladys's clucking concern was now drawing a small crowd from the depths of the modestly sized library. There was a sleepy old man from the periodicals, wide-eyed children from Juvenile, and a teenager scowling at them from the Young Adult section.

"Did you take a tumble?" Gladys asked, wringing her frail hands.

"She sure did," Red answered grimly.

"I was pushed," repeated Myrtle in a stubborn voice. "Gladys, have you seen Sybil in here? Or maybe Felix or Lucas?"

"Who?" Gladys blinked at her and Myrtle remembered that Gladys took a lot more stock in knowing book titles than remembering names. The only reason she knew Myrtle's was because she'd known her for over eighty years.

"Never mind," said Myrtle with a sigh. "What about Joan. You remember Joan, don't you?"

"Oh, I saw her in here."

"Did you?" Myrtle asked with quickening interest.

"Yes. A while ago. With little Noah, checking out some picture books." Gladys wrinkled her too-smooth-for-being elderly brow. "And you were in here, too. Don't tell me you already finished reading those two books."

"I won't then," said Myrtle. She turned to Red. "I don't know who did it, but somebody followed me here, looking for a chance to do me harm. When I walked into the library, they must have followed me, hiding behind the columns until I came out again, and then pushed me. I could have died, you know."

"No argument there," said Red. "But the rest of what you're saying sounds completely paranoid. Next, you might be claiming you're seeing spaceships or Big Foot, or the Loch Ness monster or something."

Myrtle bit her tongue, hard, to keep from firing back at him. He was going to make her lose her religion right here at the Bradley Library and Gladys would spread it all over town.

She was going to spread the fact that she fell, too. It was all thoroughly aggravating. Myrtle shot him an ugly look.

She glanced impatiently at the small crowd still gaping at her. "All right, move along. As you were. Nothing to see here." They returned to their respective areas and Myrtle said, "I'm ready to go home now."

"I'll drive you back," said Red.

Myrtle felt contrary. "I got myself here and I can get myself back. You were here running an errand or as part of your patrol, weren't you?"

Red pretended that he hadn't even heard her, but the red flush creeping up his neck told Myrtle otherwise. "Let's head to the police cruiser," he said in a clipped voice. Myrtle wondered for a moment if he were planning on handcuffing her as well.

She stiffly allowed him to hold her arm as they slowly made their way to the police car.

Myrtle wasn't in much of a talkative mood on the way back.

Red said, "Mama, if you're that off-balance, we probably need to think about getting you a walker. Or taking a closer look at Greener Pastures Retirement Home. People tell me all the time how much their folks enjoy living over there."

"I'm not off-balance," grated Myrtle. "And I *was* being careful. I was on the ramp. I won't even acknowledge *that place* you brought up."

He pulled all the way up into her driveway and hurried out to help Myrtle before she could even get out of the car. "I'm not feeble, you know," she muttered.

Red continued ignoring her, fumbling his key ring from his pocket and finding his key to her house. Myrtle kept meaning to change the locks. But it gave her the superstitious feeling that changing the locks would mean she'd promptly fall and break something and need his help.

"Why don't you lie down for a while, hmm?" asked Red absently, as he opened the door and ushered her in. "Might make you feel better. I'll get you some tea and an ibuprofen."

The whole thing made Myrtle feel very cranky. Even worse now that her arms and legs were starting to throb. "I don't want to lie down for a while."

"Can I call Trina Baker? She's an R.N. It might be nice to get her opinion."

"It would be good to have someone give an opinion that supports my assertion that I was pushed down that ramp."

Red pressed his lips shut as if keeping any errant words from flying out. He said mildly, glancing at his watch, "Except that's not what happened. All right, then. You don't want to lie down, so let's get you set up in your chair with your soap. It's almost time for it to start."

Myrtle moved slowly to her chair and sat down, nestling down into the seat. Suddenly, she did feel exhausted. Red turned her show on, and then hustled into the kitchen to get her tea and ibuprofen. The sound of growling and hissing quickly made a smile tease at the corner of her lips. Red cussed.

"Shouldn't leave your kitchen window open, Mama," he called to her. "You don't want this spawn of Satan feline in the house with you, do you?" he asked. "Let me see if I can lure it out with some tuna or something."

Before he could find any cans of tuna in the cabinet, Pasha had run into the living room, jumped up in the overstuffed armchair, and curled against her. Myrtle raised her eyebrows in surprise. Pasha was sweet with her, but this was a first. "Clever kitty," she said, stroking her softly and hearing a rumbling purr in response.

Red made a face when he saw the cat in her lap. "Haven't you been injured enough today? I don't trust that cat not to scratch or bite you if it got the idea in its head."

"Pasha wouldn't dream of it," she said. Red handed her the drink and pill and she drank it down.

Red hesitated, and then said, "While I've got you here, there was one other thing I wanted to ask you. It seems that Felix Nelson keeps turning up in our investigation and I don't know what to make of it."

Myrtle gave him an appraising look. "Is that so?"

"I even heard that you visited him in his office. I was talking to him this morning—something to do with the case—and he seemed to be trying to get me to convince you that life insurance was a good idea." Red rubbed at his forehead, looking perplexed. "I nearly laughed out loud I've got to tell you. Then he told me that you were planning on getting life insurance to help us pay for your final expenses, and I really did think he'd lost his mind. I know you're planning the cheapest funeral ever. I'm imagining that you were there doing some kind of investigating." Red gave an irritated sigh. "But try as I might, I can't figure out why you're investigating Felix."

Myrtle suddenly felt very pleased with herself. She knew something that Red didn't. She decided to wait before responding—sometimes that made Red uncomfortable and he ended up giving things away.

Sure enough, he quickly filled the silence. "I do know that Felix had a business relationship with the Whitlows."

"Did Lucas have a big policy on Cosette?" asked Myrtle.

"He sure did. She had a policy on him, too, but it wasn't nearly as big. Apparently, this was some kind of compliment that Lucas was paying Cosette—showing her how much he valued her or something." Red shrugged. "But I happen to think that a million dollar policy is a bit more than a compliment. It's a motive. Especially since the Whitlows were hurting for money. But let's get back to why you were visiting with Felix."

"Well, my final expenses. You know." She tried the pause again.

And again Red interjected into the pause. "Do you know something about Felix and the Whitlows that I don't?" She kept quiet and petted Pasha. He sighed. "I know that Felix was seen having a heated discussion with Tobin not long before he died. I'm wondering if he's also connected to Cosette in some way."

"Felix argued with Tobin? How on earth do they know each other?" asked Myrtle. But she remembered that Joan had mentioned seeing Felix, in a business suit, walking near the cemetery on the day of the funeral.

"They've probably always known each other. It's Bradley, after all. Or maybe Tobin does Felix's yard work for him. I'll find out why they argued, don't worry," said Red grimly. "And remember—it's not your job to investigate, it's mine. I do want to know why you visited Felix at his office and whether it had anything to do with Cosette's drop-in."

Myrtle paused. Red had given her a tidbit of information, so maybe she should give him one, too. It wasn't as if he were going to solve the case before she did. "The night of the party, Felix and Cosette had some sort of an argument. Sybil walked into the kitchen too late to hear what it was about. So yes, I'd say there was more going on between Felix and Cosette than life insurance. Although I don't know what, and I don't know who felt what for whom."

Red gazed steadily at his mother. "What was this argument about?"

Myrtle shook her head, frustrated. "That's the thing. Miles and I couldn't really tell what it was about. Maybe there were allegations or accusations of one kind or another leveled earlier, but by the time we were listening in, we didn't get any details."

"What was your interpretation of what you saw?" asked Red. Then he saw Myrtle balking about giving more information and he cajoled, "You always have good intuition about these things, Mama."

Red knew she had a hard time resisting praise from him. She glowed in his approval for a moment and then said, "I guess I thought that it was a love triangle of some kind. That was what seemed to make the most sense. And Sybil seems to think that Felix was worried that Cosette was acting too affectionate toward him in public."

"And Lucas wasn't in the kitchen to hear all that?" he asked.

Myrtle shook her head. "At that point, he was visiting with the guests. It wasn't until Cosette disappeared and the food and drinks obviously needed to be replaced, that he stepped in and started taking on hosting duties by going back and forth from the kitchen." Now was the time to press Red for what he might have heard about Lucas—since she hadn't gotten far with that end of the investigation. "Is he still as much of a suspect?"

Red was still mulling over what Myrtle had told him, so he was only halfway listening to her. When his guard was down, she usually could get all kinds of information from him. "He's the husband, so yes. But we haven't been able to pin anything on him. No one saw him going outside or coming back inside. No one has ever seen him have an argument with his wife. By all accounts, he was devoted to her. He did have a huge life insurance policy on Cosette, though, so that's still a little suspect. And he did have a run-in with Tobin."

Myrtle blinked at him, and then tried to cover up any surprise on her face so Red wouldn't shut down. She said casually, "Ahh. Is that because of the long-standing neighbor-feud that Cosette and Tobin had?"

"Who knows what the truth really is?" said Red with a sigh. "Tobin is dead, so he can't tell us. And Lucas just politely says that our witness to the argument misinterpreted what she saw. He says that he was in his yard and became visibly overcome with grief and Tobin came over to comfort him and that's what the witness saw."

"The witness?" asked Myrtle delicately.

"Erma." Red grinned at her. "Your favorite person."

Myrtle made a face. It seemed as if all roads led back to Erma in this case. Maybe she'd done the wrong thing by directing that cub reporter to talk with her.

"I'm going to go ahead and let you enjoy your soap, Mama. And now you need to forget about the case and leave it up to me to chase the bad guys. You're starting to look kind of puny, so be sure to rest, all right?" He snapped his fingers. "I know what. You should work on your knitting. That's a nice, peaceful activity. And you'll stay busy while you're resting."

Myrtle considered that a somewhat patronizing statement, but *was* actually feeling puny, so she let it slide. Red locked the door behind him as Myrtle fiddled with the remote until the familiar opening of *Tomorrow's Promise* came up on the screen. It looked like Kristin and her mother were at odds again while planning Kristin's twentieth wedding. At least, it seemed like Kristin's twentieth wedding. Myrtle watched until she found she could barely keep her eyes open and she gave in to a heavy sleep.

Chapter Sixteen

At some point in the middle of the night, Myrtle woke and realized she was still in her armchair and a cheery-voiced announcer was doing an infomercial in front of a very receptive studio audience. She stumbled into the bedroom, not even bothering to undress as she climbed into her bed.

The next morning, Myrtle cursed herself for not having taken an ibuprofen before returning to bed. Getting out of the bed was going to be a nightmare. But the longer she lay in bed, the more agitated she felt. It really had shaken her up to fall on that ramp. She was now feeling every single muscle in her body hurt. Myrtle felt a twinge of doubt. *Was* she too old to be investigating this murder? Everyone kept telling her that she was—maybe she should listen. She didn't feel that way yesterday, but feeling as sore as she did right now…it made her rethink everything. If she were *this* sore from a minor fall, what would a major one be like? What if she broke her hip? That would probably be enough for Red to finally persuade her to move over to Greener Pastures Retirement Home.

Myrtle sighed. It was all too dispiriting to even think about. She decided to wriggle to the side of the bed on her back, put her feet on the floor, and carefully sit up.

She'd just managed to stand when her doorbell rang. The number of visitors she was getting lately was extraordinary. Myrtle almost decided to ignore the bell, but curiosity got the better of her.

She peered out the front window and saw Erma's face leering back at her. She jumped back from the window. People could see through that white curtain? Or was Erma simply trying to mess with her head? Myrtle had half a mind not to open the door. But Red had mentioned that Erma might have information about an argument between Tobin and Lucas. She hesitated, and then slowly unlocked the door.

"Myrtle," said Erma, sweeping inside and clutching her throat dramatically. "I nearly had a heart attack—a real heart attack like my father used to have. He had quadruple bypass surgery, did I tell you that? I think I might have gotten his genes because sometimes I feel like my heart skips beats."

Myrtle could have told her that mitral valve prolapse, which sounded very much like Erma's ailment, had nothing to do with heart attacks, but she knew Erma wouldn't listen to her. She headed to her armchair with Erma crooning along behind her.

"So when I saw my poor dear old neighbor on the front page of the paper this morning, my heart skipped more than one beat. It must have skipped fifty! I think I nearly kicked the bucket right there on my front walkway."

Pity she'd recovered so completely. Myrtle scowled. "What? Front page of what? Me?"

Erma had an expression of horrified delight on her face. "You mean you don't know? Could you not? Is that possible? Oh, but that's right—your paper was still on the front walk."

"It's not only possible, it's true." Myrtle struggled out of the chair. "Excuse me while I retrieve my paper."

"I brought it for you." Erma looked vaguely around her, then snapped her fingers and reached into her shiny patent-leather pocketbook. "Here it is."

Myrtle snatched it away from her and gazed in horror at the headline. *Bradley Matriarch Tumbles Down Library Stairs,* by Kim McKenzie.

Erma was babbling on. "Those young people, they keep on top of things, don't they! How did Kim hear about your fall when I didn't know about it and I live right next door to you? I can see you're all right, thank goodness, although that's a nasty purple bruise on your arm."

Myrtle's arm started throbbing on cue.

"It reminds me of a bruise I got one time when I ran into a stop sign. You know how the town was real lackadaisical about stop signs for a while. Then they put one up out of the blue, and I was taking my usual stroll and ran smack into it. Bruised me up real good. The bruise was blue, then it turned sort of a green, then it was...."

Myrtle was desperate not to hear the details of Erma's collision with the road sign. She interrupted, "I didn't fall down the stairs. I was pushed down the ramp." She recognized the mulish tone in her voice, but couldn't stop herself. That silly cub reporter had it all wrong. It was most annoying to be thought of as the kind of old lady who was sloppy enough to pitch down some stairs.

Erma's rodent-like eyes got as large as they could get. "Did you hit your head when you fell?" Erma was never one for subtlety.

"I did *not*. I'm not imagining this, Erma. I felt a hand at my back and I was pushed."

"Well then." Erma seemed abruptly at a loss for words. But that lasted only nanoseconds. "Why do you think you were pushed?"

"Because I'm getting closer to finding out who is responsible for these murders. And when I do, there'll *really* be a good headline in the *Bradley Bugle*. Because I'll write the best investigative story ever. I started writing it just the other night."

Erma squinted at her.

Myrtle sighed. "Erma, since you're here, there's something I wanted to ask you about. Red mentioned that you might have seen Tobin and Lucas arguing."

Erma grinned wide enough at her that Myrtle was able to spot several fillings. "I didn't *see* them arguing. I *heard* them arguing. Well, I saw that they were having a real intense discussion, so I rolled down my car windows. Out of curiosity, you know."

"Tobin wasn't consoling Lucas over the death of Cosette?" asked Myrtle.

"Far from it. Lucas was furious. He was waving his hands around and yelling at Tobin that he was always mean to Cosette. And something-something about garbage, which I couldn't really catch." Erma frowned with frustration. "Anyhow, the point was that Lucas was mad, mad, mad. I've never seen him mad, have you? Not even when Cosette would treat him like crud, which she did all the time. Maybe he killed Tobin."

Maybe. But it seemed more likely to Myrtle that Lucas would have lashed out at Tobin in the heat of the moment—not following him over to a cemetery to surreptitiously murder him on the very morning of his wife's funeral. But who knew?

"That was all you heard?" asked Myrtle. "You didn't hear what Tobin was saying back to him?"

Erma's face got splotchy. "It wasn't for lack of trying. But I was driving the car and was already only going five miles an hour. It would have been too obvious if I'd completely stopped to hear what Tobin was saying. He looked angry. Had his arms crossed in front of him and it looked like he was yelling."

"Red told me that Lucas said he was being comforted by Tobin."

Erma gave her braying laugh in response.

"All right, I have another question for you. You left Cosette's drop-in pretty early, didn't you?"

Erma quieted and nodded. "Had some terrible heartburn that night. I had this dip. Ugh. It was the worst dip in the world. Spinach and artichoke, but it was weird tasting. Made me feel sick, so I went home."

Myrtle shifted uncomfortably in her seat. "There were several of those dips that night, weren't there?"

Erma shook her head emphatically. "Nope. Just the one. Nasty stuff. Heartburn and nausea. Bleh."

Myrtle at least had the distinct sense of satisfaction that she'd made Erma Sherman nauseated. "Anyway. When you left the party, who did you see on the way out? Anyone arriving, or leaving early?"

Erma squinted in thought. "Saw Sybil and Felix leaving."

That fit with what Sybil was saying. "So they left together."

"Nope. Left in separate cars with Sybil telling Felix how much she loved him and Felix looking like he wanted to disappear ASAP," said Erma, chortling.

"How did Felix look?"

"Mad," said Erma. "And Sybil looked fit to be tied that Felix wasn't telling her he loved her back." She gave a leering grin.

"Anybody else?" Erma stared at her, so Myrtle elaborated. "Did you see Cosette's daughter, Joan, there?"

"Oh sure. Saw her going around the side of the house."

Myrtle took in a quick breath. "This didn't surprise you? The drop-in wasn't an outdoor party."

Erma shrugged. "The front door was totally blocked up with people. I figured she didn't want to try to elbow her way through the crowd. And I knew her little guy was there. Thought she was trying to pick him back up and leave again."

That seemed to be all the information that Myrtle was going to be able to squeeze from Erma. She now needed to get rid of her as quickly as she possibly could. "Erma, I'm pretty worn out now. I'd probably better go put my feet up again. I'll see you soon, I'm sure." Unless Myrtle caught sight of Erma *first*.

After Erma was dispatched, Myrtle headed into the kitchen to make herself a strong coffee. She'd used to love coffee in her youth, but as she got older, it tended to upset her stomach a bit. Still, this morning required a cup of the strongest stuff she could handle. She dug out her half-and-half, put the sugar bowl on the table, and then poured herself a cup. Myrtle had even made a full pot of the stuff. She figured she might need it.

Myrtle sat down at her kitchen table and doctored the coffee with sugar and cream. Her eyebrows shot up as she had a cautious sip. She'd certainly be fully awake now. She coughed.

Myrtle caught some movement out of the corner of her eye and jerked her head in that direction, heart thumping. She relaxed wnen she saw Miles peering through the back window at her.

Myrtle quickly let him in. "Are you trying to scare me out of my wits?"

Miles looked repentant. "No. I was making sure you were up and about. I didn't want to knock on the door and drag you out of bed to come let me in. So I thought I'd check through the window to see if I saw you."

"I might not even have been dressed respectably," said Myrtle, feeling grouchy.

Miles must have been biting his tongue, because he didn't mention the fact that she frequently visited him in the middle of the night while she was dressed in a nightgown.

"I'm guessing you're here because of the story," said Myrtle, blowing out a hefty sigh.

Miles pulled out the paper from under his arm. "Have you seen it? *Bradley Matriarch...."*

"Yes, I've seen it," said Myrtle, cutting him off. "A ridiculous piece of journalism, even for Bradley, North Carolina. Seriously, with a murderer running around slashing down half the town, all you can think of to write about is someone's fall. And she didn't even get the story *right*. It wasn't even a *fall*! If she'd gotten *that* part right, it would have been much more of a story. And it wasn't on the stairs, it was on the ramp."

"You didn't fall?" Miles's gaze fell on Myrtle's bruised arm.

"I was pushed."

Miles stared at her. "Pushed. You're sure."

"Of course I'm sure! I could hardly mistake the feeling of a hand on my back, shoving me."

Miles asked, "You're not just covering up the fact that you're not as steady on your feet as you used to be, are you?"

"Certainly not! And I'm very steady on my feet. Besides, I don't do anything stupid. I don't reach for things on the floor. I don't try to run. I wear sensible shoes. I. Was. *Pushed*!" Myrtle was flushed and feeling defensive now. If one more person presumed that she'd made the story up, she was sure she was going to scream. And she felt that uncertain, dispiriting sensation of age pressing down on her again.

"Who do you think would do such a thing?"

"All of them. Any of them," said Myrtle with a wide wave of her hand.

"Of them?"

"The suspects, Miles! Pay attention. Who else would shove me down the ramp?"

Miles could think of a few people who might be tempted from time to time. Myrtle's own son would likely make the short list.

"Any one of the suspects is a likely candidate. If someone is capable of murder, he's capable of silencing someone who is getting too close to the truth." As Miles stared blankly at her, she said impatiently, "Me. Me, Miles."

"Have you found out anything new? Because from what I remember of the information you'd gathered, it shouldn't be anything to put your life in danger."

"It doesn't seem to be that way to me either. Joan returned to her mother's house, although she swears she didn't. She was even seen sneaking around the side of the house. Sybil didn't leave with Felix at all—they were in separate cars, so they can't give each other alibis. Sybil admits that Felix and Cosette had a real argument—nothing about Congress, either, although she's not exactly sure what it was about. Maybe Sybil came directly back to Cosette's and struck her over the head with the mallet out of anger. Lucas had a heated argument with Tobin. Joan says she definitely saw Tobin early on the morning he died." She shrugged. "That's a lot of facts I'm armed with. Somebody thinks I'm dangerous."

The doorbell rang and Myrtle rolled her eyes. "You'd think I had a revolving door on the front of my house."

"Here, I'll get it," said Miles.

"People will say we're in love," said Myrtle dryly. "Let's hope it's not loud-mouthed Erma again. She's convinced we spend every waking moment together."

Miles cautiously looked out. Myrtle knew he had no desire for a visit with Erma Sherman either. "Oh. It's that cub reporter."

"Tina?"

"I think her name is Kim," said Miles, looking back at Myrtle.

"Whatever."

"Are you receiving guests?" asked Miles formally.

"Let her in. I have an idea." Miles turned to let her in and Myrtle grabbed her knitting from the cardboard box on a kitchen chair.

Myrtle decided that her first impression of Kim at the funeral was a pretty accurate one. Although Kim seemed to cultivate a fluffy, innocuous appearance with her strand of pearls, long blonde hair, and headband, Myrtle noticed again that her eyes were mean. She remembered this look on many a bully's face from her school teaching days. If there was one thing those days had taught her, it was that she couldn't stand a bully.

Myrtle beamed at Kim. "Come on in, my dear. Can I get you some milk and cookies?"

Kim gave a hard smile, which didn't reach her eyes. "No thanks. I came to get a follow-up for my story. How are you doing? People apparently want to know, so Sloan called me to get in touch with you." She didn't bother to disguise the bored tone in her voice.

"Oh, I'm doing just fine," said Myrtle sweetly.

Miles frowned. "Myrtle, didn't you want to tell Kim…."

He was determined to tell about the pushing, Myrtle could tell. She interrupted him. "About that interesting conversation I had with Red? Why yes. Yes, I did."

Myrtle ignored Miles's furrowed brow and said, "I'm sure you're sick to death already of that silly story about my falling."

Kim looked rather discomfited and Myrtle suspected that she'd hit the bulls-eye. "No. Well, a little. But it's a small town. Apparently people here are interested in stories that wouldn't be printed in other papers."

"Wouldn't you much rather be working on that big story? The murders?"

Kim's mean eyes gleamed. "Of course. But there's no more information being released right now. Wait. You're the police chief's mother, right?"

Myrtle gritted her teeth at being described that way. "Yes, I am. Of course, Red tries to be very careful about releasing information. But you'd understand if he lets things slip from time to time."

"It would be only natural," agreed Kim, still in that forced pleasant tone. Then she frowned. "I thought Sloan mentioned that you had plans on reporting this story yourself, Mrs. Clover."

"Me?" Myrtle released a gale of trilling laughter that made Miles's jaw drop. "Sloan is such a joker. He knows that it's all I can do to keep up with that helpful hints column every week." She felt a slight pang as she realized it was actually time to turn in another column and she'd completely forgotten. "Perhaps he's flattering me, trying to butter me up. I was his English teacher once, you know."

"So what information was it that Chief Clover provided you?" asked Kim, cutting to the chase in a hard voice.

"Well, apparently there was a witness to the murder at the cemetery. Since it was all out in the open on public property, you know. This witness loves to come get the pecans from the trees in the cemetery. Have you noticed the lovely pecan trees there?" asked Myrtle innocently.

Kim shot her an impatient look. "No, I haven't. So the witness was in the cemetery and had information on a suspect? Not enough to make an arrest, apparently."

"Oh, I wouldn't know that. But since there haven't been any arrests, then I would suppose not, would you?"

Kim was snapping open her tiny purse and pulling out a tiny notebook and pencil. Myrtle felt a twinge of purse envy.

Her own pocketbooks were monstrous things. She'd tried to carry something smaller, but had found smaller bags did her no good because she wouldn't have the things she needed at hand. Still, seeing a pert pocketbook like Kim's made her sigh.

Pencil poised over the pad, Kim looked expectantly at Myrtle. "What is the name and address of this witness? Did Chief Clover tell you that?"

Myrtle was warm with satisfaction. "It's Darla Covington. She loves to get pecans to sell at the farmer's market along with her corn, tomatoes, and okra. She lives on a farm on County Road Five."

Miles gave her a reproving look. "That's pretty far away, Myrtle. She's a young woman traveling alone."

Kim gave Miles a disdainful look down her small nose. "What an old-fashioned view, Mister….I've forgotten your name. I'm doing a job and sometimes I have to be alone. I'm safe in Bradley, I promise you. If I *don't* feel safe?" She opened the small bag again and held it to show off its contents to Myrtle and Miles. There was a rather prissy-looking gun sitting demurely in the bottom of the purse.

"Don't worry about me. I'll be fine." Kim looked smug.

In Myrtle's experience, smugness usually meant that the person feeling it was in a lot more trouble than they thought. "Miles is right, dear. You should take Sloan with you out there." Which would serve Sloan right, handing over her story to this young woman. "You just never know. But talk to Darla. See what she saw that morning. Maybe you can crack the big story."

Kim's eyes gleamed. She must be dying to get out of Bradley. But she needed a big story to get a job at a paper in a larger town. Kim stood up and walked toward Myrtle's front door. "Don't bother getting up," she called behind her without even turning her head. "I can find my way out. I'll write a follow-up story that you're feeling fine, Mrs. Clover."

Miles's gaze fell on a folder that Kim had left on the table. His hand reached for the folder as he opened his mouth. He snapped his mouth shut again as Myrtle stretched out and slapped his hand hard.

"Bye-bye, Kim!" sang out Myrtle.

Chapter Seventeen

After the girl left, Myrtle picked up the folder. "Go lock that door, Miles. With any luck, she won't remember this folder until tomorrow. I can say it must have fallen off the table and underneath where I couldn't see it."

Myrtle opened the folder as Miles walked back from locking the door. "Wait a minute," said Miles. "There are no pecans yet. Those are harvested in late fall here, aren't they?"

Myrtle said, "She wasn't going to know any better. It was all she could do to rein in her impatience enough to even have a conversation with me. Disdainful little miss. No, I made it all up, of course. Tina was getting underfoot and it was time to get her out of the way for a while. Couldn't keep tripping over her while she was getting constant updates on my stupid fall."

"It's Kim. Not Tina. Is there even a Darla Covington out there?"

"Of course there is! And Darla will give her what-for, let me assure you. Little Miss Thing won't know whether she's coming or going after that." Myrtle shuffled through the papers in the folder.

"What's in there?" asked Miles. "And do you mind if I help myself to some coffee?"

"Go right ahead," said Myrtle absently. "And—a lot of random pictures and notes."

"Pictures?" Miles poured himself a generous cup of coffee.

"Yes. The kind of pictures that look like they've been printed off a computer. It looks like what's-her-name was trying to take a bunch of pictures in the hopes that something she shot on film would be important or related to a story. Thank goodness she didn't arrive during the aftermath of my fall." The idea of a picture of herself sprawled across the library ramp made Myrtle shudder.

Miles took a long sip of his coffee, then made a horrible face and coughed. "How strong did you make this stuff? Could it possibly be lethal?"

"Don't be a baby. I was simply trying to wake up this morning." Myrtle gestured to her empty cup. "I drank all of mine."

Miles was still coughing. "This is going to put hair on my chest," he gasped.

"Silly." Myrtle got to the last couple of pictures in the folder and paused. "Now this is interesting. I guess Kim must have been trying to take a picture of this cat hunting a bird. But look what's in the far corner!"

Miles took the picture away from Myrtle. "That's Sybil, isn't it? Talking to Tobin? Is that the day he died?"

"Not according to the timestamp on the photo. But Sybil acted like she had no idea who Tobin was, remember? And here she is engaged in conversation with him."

"Engaged in conversation?" Miles squinted at the photo again. "Isn't that a bit of a stretch? It seems more like they're having some sort of brief encounter of some kind. Maybe he's asking her what time it is."

Myrtle snatched back the photo. "She's not wearing a watch."

"She could check her cell phone and see the time. I'm only pointing out that it's possible that this wasn't something at all memorable and perhaps she had no idea who the guy even was. Then, when you asked her about Tobin, she *did* give you a blank look because she didn't know the man's name she was speaking to." Miles voice was incredibly reasonable. She hated it when he sounded reasonable.

"Maybe," grumbled Myrtle, still staring at the picture. "Just the same, I think I'll ask Sybil about it."

"When are you planning on seeing Sybil again? I could go with you."

Myrtle said, "I don't know. I'm feeling all out of sorts now." She drew in her lip when she realized she was pouting, but felt at least that she was owning the emotion. Why shouldn't she be out of sorts? Getting shoved, folks lying to her, constant visitors to her dusty home that Puddin didn't have the skill to clean properly? It was all most vexing.

The doorbell rang and Myrtle groaned. "Welcome to Myrtle Clover's bar and grill. Do you have a reservation?"

Miles knit his brows. "Usually you're happy to see visitors." He hurried up to peep out the window and back to report, "Especially when suspects are at the door. Lucas, Joan, and Noah are here…bearing food, too."

Myrtle brightened. "Guess they're returning the casseroles with food in them." Her face darkened again. "Unless it's poisoned. Because it could be. They might have flung me down the ramp yesterday."

"I'm letting them in," said Miles with determination. "And I think you need to try to shake this mood. It's most unlike you, Myrtle."

Myrtle stuck her tongue out at his back as he strode to the door, and then looked as demure as possible as he let Lucas and Joan in. She even picked up her knitting to play the fluffy old lady role again. Of course, it sort of gave her away that she didn't even have a row of knitting done. She really needed to have Elaine come by with some finished projects so that Myrtle could pretend she'd just started a new one.

Noah ran in and up to Myrtle. "Cookies?" he asked hopefully, looking for the jar on her counter.

"Of course! If it's all right with your mama," said Myrtle sweetly. "And what do y'all have for me? Casseroles? What a treat!"

Joan put her casserole in the fridge and took the one from her father and stuck it in there, as well. She pushed her mousy hair out of her eyes and peered at Myrtle through her thick glasses, examining her. "Well, we couldn't simply return the dishes empty after we'd read in the paper this morning about your spill."

"Terrifying," said Lucas, looking at Myrtle with concern as he walked in to join them. His limp didn't seem so bad today. "Did it scare you to pieces?"

Myrtle thought back to the moment she'd started falling and shivered. Actually, it *had* scared her. Which made her mad. She hated being scared. She made a decision: instead of feeling despair from the fall, she'd feel anger. Anger could be a powerful motivator for Myrtle—and she really didn't like feeling depressed.

Joan glanced across and accurately read the expression on Myrtle's face. "Of course it scared her to pieces. At least you're all right. Here you are, knitting away, safe and sound."

As if on cue, Myrtle started making knitting motions again with her needles. It was amazing that she could even remember as much about knitting as she did. Must be muscle memory. "Safe and sound…and now well-fed, too. So considerate of y'all to bring food."

"It's something for lunch and something for supper. I put reheating instructions on the tops of the casseroles. Noah, only two cookies," said Joan sternly, wagging two stubby fingers at the child to illustrate.

"Won't you have some cookies too, Joan? Or Lucas?"

Lucas shook his head and Joan looked ruefully down at her round form, which she'd unsuccessfully tried to hide with a baggy sweat suit. "I'd better pass on cookies, Miss Myrtle. But thanks."

Myrtle beamed at Joan and then turned to Lucas and said teasingly, "I didn't know you could cook."

His broad face colored. He said, "I can't. But Joan does an amazing job so she cooked for the both of us. I was eating high on the hog when Hazel was staying with me. Didn't realize how good I had it," he said with a sigh. "But she had to go back home, of course, and Joan has been sweet to help me out. Cosette was such a wonderful cook," he said wistfully, patting his generous stomach.

Myrtle noticed that he misted up, but at least didn't seem quite as distraught as he had before.

Joan watched him with a solicitous eye, apparently concerned he might suddenly get very mushy. Noah chirped, "Milk?"

"Of course! We definitely need some milk to wash our cookies down," said Myrtle.

"I'll get it," said Miles, looking glad to have something to do. He wasn't wonderful with emotions and was likely just as worried as Joan that Lucas was suddenly going to tear up.

"Are you feeling all right, then?" asked Joan as Noah gulped down the milk that Miles handed him. "Not too sore?"

"I'm pretty sore today," admitted Myrtle. "But then, that's to be expected."

"I think you're very lucky," said Lucas. "Falls can be a terrible thing." He looked out the window. "Do you enjoy living on the lake side of the street?"

"I used to when I was younger and when Red was growing up. Sometimes I'll still go down to the dock and sit and look at the water. I have a rocking chair down there. I sold the boat to Red since I figured my boating days are over. He takes it out sometimes to fish. And Jack likes the boat, of course."

Lucas walked over to the window and looked out into Myrtle's backyard. "You have some nice shade here, too. I bet it helps you keep your air conditioning costs down in the summer."

"I do like the shade. And the yard looks pretty good, despite having Dusty as the yardman." She snorted. "Although my gardenias are looking kind of puny right now. They're turning yellow and dropping leaves."

Lucas turned to look in the direction of the bushes. "I'm sorry to hear that. Looks like whiteflies. You should call Dusty up and tell him that he needs to spray the bushes the next time he's here."

"He'll probably pass out from surprise that I'm asking him to do anything other than prune, cut grass, or weed trim," said Myrtle dryly. "Well, if he won't do it, then Red can."

Miles said, "I should get your opinion on my own bushes. They don't look so hot either. And I'm no fan of commercial insecticides, so I don't even know what I could do about them if it's whiteflies."

"How environmentally conscious of you, Miles!" said Myrtle, raising her eyebrows at him.

"Well, whatever I spray in my yard will eventually wash down into the lake, right?" Miles shrugged. "I doubt we want to drink that, that's all."

"I can take a look, if you want." said Lucas. "Want to walk over there real quickly while Joan and Noah have a short visit? Maybe I can remember what to put in a homemade, natural insecticide."

As they left, Joan said, "That was nice of Miles to do that. Dad needs the distraction."

Myrtle said, "I'm glad to see that he's out of the house. I'm sure it's got to be good for him to see people."

"I think so. He's having a hard time adjusting to life without Mother. His tendency is to want to stay inside and mope. I have to keep calling him up with ideas for getting out and visiting folks," said Joan, taking a napkin to Noah's chocolate-covered face.

"It's a shame," said Myrtle. She pretended to idly pick at the checkered tablecloth. "And such a pity that he's having to be without your mother. You must have wracked your brain trying to think of what you might have seen."

She glanced up in time to see Joan watching her intensely behind her thick lenses. Joan said, "Of course. Although Mother and I were definitely not close, I would want to help the police with their investigation as much as possible."

This all sounded rather rehearsed to Myrtle. She pressed a little harder. "You know, I was talking with my neighbor this morning and she mentioned seeing you return to the party that awful night. Sybil, of course, had mentioned it to me too, but having Erma corroborate that fact…" Myrtle shrugged.

Joan opened her mouth, apparently to protest, and then snapped it closed again. She and Myrtle watched as Noah rearranged Myrtle's refrigerator magnets and talked quietly to himself.

"You're right," said Joan, after heaving a sigh. "I did return to the drop-in. But it's not what you're thinking. I had second thoughts after I left. Mother drove me nuts and made me furious. She was pushy and treated me as if I were still a kid. But she really cared about me and about Noah—although she never showed it in the right ways. After I cooled off a while at the store and at home, I realized I owed somebody an apology. Actually, I was thinking that I owed it to Noah."

"But you were seen going around the side of the house," said Myrtle. "Noah was inside in a bedroom."

Joan shot Myrtle a slightly annoyed look. "That's right. But you have to remember back to that night. Mother had invited most of the town to come over and many of them had shown up. That small house was so crowded that it was hard to move through it. Even if I *had* decided to push my way through, people would have stopped me to talk every few feet. Besides, there were a lot of people blocking the front door."

"So you walked around the back…."

"….and I saw my mother on the ground." Joan stopped and seemed to be considering her words carefully. She glanced back over at Noah, but he was still absorbed in the magnets and not listening at all. "I know this sounds cold. I didn't wish my mother ill. I did start to go to her, but she was so still that it seemed as if I were already too late to do anything to help. Then, when I heard your voice going into the yard, I turned around and left." She slumped in her chair. "I knew Dad was there and that the sitter was still with Noah."

"You went back home?" asked Myrtle.

"I did. I think I was almost in a daze. I know I shouldn't have done any of that. I should have run to Mother, checked for a pulse. I should have dialed the police or called an ambulance. I should have alerted everyone at the drop-in. I should have gone to Noah and taken him to a quieter, less-confusing place. But I didn't."

"Why didn't you?"

"Because I knew how it would look. I had to be one of the top suspects. Everyone knew how I talked about Mother. And I was conveniently on the scene. I started thinking about Noah and how awful it would be for him if I ended up going to prison—even though I hadn't even done anything. I left."

Myrtle gave her an assessing look. It was something of a believable story…but then, wouldn't she try her best to make it be so?

"Potty!" proclaimed Noah, abruptly pausing in his magnet redecoration.

"Do you need to go potty?" asked Joan, giving Myrtle an apologetic smile.

"That's fine. The potty is right down the hall there." Myrtle stood up and peered out the window as Joan got up to escort Noah. "Miles sure is talking your father's ear off about his shrubs. I didn't realize your dad knew so much about gardening."

Joan shot her a swift look that Myrtle couldn't read. "He knows lots about many things," she said.

Noah and Joan walked down the short hall as Miles and Lucas came back in. Miles was looking pleased.

"Did you find out the spray you need to use?" asked Myrtle.

"I sure did. If I have any left over, I'll give it to you."

"Don't give it to me…give it to Dusty. With any luck, he'll know what to do with it," said Myrtle. She sighed. "And if he doesn't, then I hope I can find a half-decent yardman to take his place. It's the hardest thing in the world to find a yardman in Bradley. And we lost a pretty good one when Tobin died."

Lucas shifted uncomfortably and Myrtle noticed that he wasn't meeting her gaze.

"Of course, you might not have agreed that Tobin was a good yardman…or a good anything. A neighbor of mine mentioned that she saw you and Tobin arguing before he died," said Myrtle. "Did y'all come to odds over some yard work he'd done for you?"

"Oh, no, Tobin never did yard work for us. We had Tiny come by ever so often to do all the hard labor in the yard. And then Cosette was the one who planted flowers and did the decorative part."

Tiny was actually a giant of a man. But the South was full of names like that. "And Cosette purchased the croquet set, I suppose," said Myrtle.

"She would have, yes. I suppose she bought the set for whenever she had parties."

"So, if Tobin didn't do any work for you, then what might you have been arguing about?" asked Myrtle.

Lucas sighed. "I hated to speak ill of the dead. And I guess I didn't want to look any more suspicious than I already did. But I was taking out the trash, and Tobin made sort of a snide comment about Cosette—something like he was glad that now things would at least be a lot quieter on our street. I must have had a lot of pent-up emotions, because I really let him have it. Now I feel just terrible about that."

Joan and Noah came back in and Joan gave Lucas a quizzical look. Then she said, "I think we should run along now. The instructions are on the casseroles, Miss Myrtle, as I mentioned before. Dad is looking tired and you must be pooped, yourself."

"I'm all right, since I slept in so late this morning. But I'll probably sleep well tonight," said Myrtle.

Miles snorted and Myrtle glared at him. Well, she *might* sleep well tonight.

After Joan, Noah, and Lucas left, Miles sat back down at the kitchen table with Myrtle. "So what did you make of all that?"

"It sounds like they were covering up for themselves, because they didn't want their actions to be misinterpreted by the police," said Myrtle. "But they might just as well be lying. What it boils down to is, that Lucas had an argument with Tobin, and Joan returned to the party and walked around the side of the house. The rest of their stories could be totally made up."

There was a tap on Myrtle's front door and she groaned. "Go away!"

Miles got up and walked to the door. "I'm starting to think you should place an ad in the *Bugle* for a butler," he noted. He looked out the window. "It's Red."

"I suppose we should let him in," said Myrtle.

"He seems to be carrying…an object," said Miles slowly.

"Well, let him in so he can put it down." Honestly, sometimes Miles seemed to need as much direction as a child.

Miles obediently opened the door. "Hi, Red."

Red came in carrying a folded walker. Myrtle shrieked, putting a hand to her heart.

Chapter Eighteen

"It's time for me to be getting home," muttered Miles before making a speedy exit.

Some friend.

"Red, get that thing away from me. Return it to the store at once. It's a waste of your money. I'm not using it. I don't need a walker."

Red sighed. "Are you done? Spit out all your reasons for not wanting one? Good. First of all, I didn't buy this walker. Carolyn Frances gave it to me straight out. Said her mama didn't need it anymore."

"Because her mama is dead! Who knows, maybe she tripped over the walker while trying to use it and that's what killed her. I don't want the thing. I don't like it," Myrtle glared at the offending walker.

"You're being hardheaded. There's nothing wrong with needing to stay a bit steadier on your feet. In my way of thinking, this walker will help you to stay independent longer," said Red.

Myrtle stood up and walked very steadily to the coffeepot to pour herself another cup of coffee. Then she walked back, perfectly balanced. "I'm independent enough now. I hate those walkers. They squeak. And they're too hard to push."

Red opened up a plastic bag that he had hanging on his arm. "That's why I brought these." He held up a bag of tennis balls. "We're going to put these tennis balls on the back legs of the walker and you'll glide around like a swan."

"I don't *want* to glide around like a swan. I want to thump around with my cane." Myrtle felt her face color. This whole issue would give her an apoplectic fit. Carolyn Frances. Interfering biddy.

Red ignored her and put the tennis balls on the walker legs, talking as he did. "I think you'll find that you get used to the walker and that it gives you more stability and more options as far as where you go."

"It's a waste. And waste is sinful, Red. You should give that walker to an elderly person who needs it."

"Mama, *you* are elderly. Very, very elderly."

"Didn't say I wasn't. Said that you should give the walker to an elderly person who *needs* it. I don't. And a walker is absolutely no help when someone deliberately pushes you down a ramp."

Red looked up at his mother. "That's another thing, Mama. You don't need to go around town telling everyone that story about someone shoving you down the library ramp. It only makes you look silly."

"It's the truth! And I've never looked silly a day in my life."

"I've got Trina Balmer coming by tomorrow to show you how to use the walker. Apparently, it does take training, because improper use can make seniors fall down."

Myrtle gritted her teeth. She had a feeling that she was going to be indisposed when Trina Balmer came by the next day.

"And make sure you open the door to Trina. She's going out of her way to help you train on the walker as a favor to me," said Red smoothly. He stood up and took a few experimental steps with the device. "Yes, I can see that it's not really intuitive. Training will help." He leaned over to give his mother a peck on the cheek before she could turn away. "Okay, that's it. I've got to run follow up on a couple of leads. I'll see you later, Mama."

A few minutes later, a walker-free Myrtle was busily dragging gnomes out of her storage shed and placing them on her front lawn in plain view of Red's house. A walker deserved a lot more gnomes, actually, but Myrtle was going to have to pace herself. She was still sore from the fall yesterday.

She was resting against a woodcutter gnome when Sybil drove up in her 1970s Chevy Caprice. She parked in Myrtle's driveway and gave her a jaunty wave. She hopped out of the car and opened the back door to reach in the back seat. When Sybil came around the side of the car toward Myrtle, she was toting a gnome. She grinned at Myrtle, white teeth gleaming in her tanned face.

"Well, look at you!" she called. "You sure seem in fine fettle. Here I was all worried about you after reading that newspaper article."

Myrtle made a dismissive gesture at the mention of the article. "Shoddy journalism," she said with a sniff. "What have you got there?"

"A little feel-better present for you. I love trolling flea markets and yard sales to find things for my collections. So I went out early this morning after I got the paper and found this guy." Sybil held him out so that Myrtle could see him. It was a gnome in perfect condition. Even better—he was sticking out his tongue in glee. A very animated specimen.

Myrtle beamed at Sybil. "I love him. May I pay you for him?"

Sybil shook her head. "He was ridiculously cheap. The woman was practically giving him away. Where do you want me to put him?"

Myrtle surveyed her front yard. "How about right there? In the front. Point him directly at Red's house."

She watched with satisfaction as Sybil carefully placed the irreverent gnome right where he could give Red the sassiest view. "Perfect!"

Sybil walked back up to Myrtle. "Say, you do look tired, Miss Myrtle. Are you done putting gnomes out? If you're not, then I can help you while you go inside."

"I think your gnome put the finishing touch on the yard, Sybil. Can you stay for a glass of tea? It's gotten right warm out here and we should cool off for a minute."

Sybil followed Myrtle in, holding the door for her. "Wait…you've got a walker now? When did that happen?"

Myrtle scowled at the offending device. "Red was interfering. Being overprotective as usual. I don't need a walker. I have this." She picked up her cane and swung it in the air.

Sybil stared at the walker. "My mother has a walker, actually. I think she likes the fact that she can hang a bag on it and carry things around with her easier."

"That's what a pocketbook is for," said Myrtle. "I have a large pocketbook that I hang on my shoulder and I manage perfectly well with my cane."

Sybil must have heard the agitation that Myrtle couldn't seem to suppress and dropped the subject. "Knitting? Are you knitting now, too? I must not be paying attention in book club."

"No, I'm not really knitting. That was Elaine's idea. Red and Elaine try to keep me busy, you know." She looked at the knitting paraphernalia. "I don't know, maybe I could knit a little. Sometimes I'm restless or can't sleep. My automatic reaction to it is *no*, though. Makes me feel like an old lady."

Sybil said, "Believe it or not, but I know several knitters and not a single one is an old lady. One is a teenager as a matter of fact. And Elaine isn't old. Not even close. Is Elaine knitting, too?"

This was true. It sparked a bit more interest in Myrtle. "She is. Hmm. Well, maybe I could look into it. Maybe I simply don't like the skeins that Elaine brought over."

"There's a knitting shop right in downtown Bradley," said Sybil helpfully.

Myrtle narrowed her eyes suspiciously at Sybil. "You're not in league with Elaine and Red are you? On the Keep-Mama-Out-Of-Trouble campaign?"

Sybil gave her hooting laugh. "Not a bit. And I'm surprised you didn't notice that shop, yourself. You're usually the eagle-eyed one, aren't you?"

"I wouldn't have noticed a craft shop, even if it were painted with purple polka-dots," said Myrtle. She sighed. "Okay. I'll at least go shop there and see what I think. It might be boring enough to make me fall back asleep some of these wakeful nights."

But Sybil had lost interest in the conversation. She was holding a printed photo—the picture that Myrtle had swiped from the cub reporter's folder. It was shaking in her hand a little. "Ah. Yes, the young reporter from the *Bugle*, she of the shoddy journalism, left that here." A bit of a fib.

Sybil stared at the picture. "Why would she take a picture like this? And why would she leave it here?"

"Those are good questions," said Myrtle, shifting in her chair. As soon as she thought up an answer for the second one, she'd give it. "Why would she *take* that picture? She's new to the town, looking for news, and has apparently been going around and snapping pictures to see what she can stir up. Not exactly the best way to track down stories, but she'll learn. I suppose."

"Why do you have the picture?"

Myrtle heaved another sigh. Now she really was feeling tired. "It was an accident—she didn't realize she'd left it here. I was interested in the photo, actually. You'd told me that you didn't even know who Tobin was, and there you are having a conversation with him in that photo. It's kind of curious, isn't it?"

Sybil studied Myrtle with the same caution as she had the picture. "I suppose it is."

Myrtle cleared her throat. "I was thinking about reasons someone might deny knowing someone. There really are a lot, you know…I hadn't realized until I started brainstorming them. One of the things I came up with is that you were worried about being a suspect again. You're already a suspect in one murder."

Sybil nodded, hoop earrings swinging as she did.

Myrtle continued, "You obviously love collecting things. As I recall, Tobin was a collector himself. He lived alone and had a big baseball card collection—he mentioned it to me before he died. He squabbled a lot with Cosette because I think he was bored, and maybe a little lonely."

Sybil looked a bit teary and nodded again.

Myrtle took a deep breath. "You found a common bond with Tobin. You also enjoy collecting things. Maybe Tobin came over to do some yard work for you and you got to talking. You were also bored. You were also lonely."

Sybil was listening intently.

"And you found some comfort in each other," said Myrtle simply.

"Comfort," said Sybil nodding. "Yes."

"But when you met Felix and started going on dates with him, you were completely taken with him. He was smart and financially successful. He seemed to balance you out better than Tobin did. Perhaps you were even a little embarrassed by Tobin and didn't want to spend your life as the wife of a yardman," suggested Myrtle.

"Oh, I don't think that's true," rebutted Sybil quickly. Then she paused. "Maybe. Maybe there was *some* snobbery there. Also, I don't think a relationship with him would have worked for the long run." She flushed. "That probably sounds bad."

"Not really. It's not as if you and Tobin signed some sort of contract for a relationship. But I'm guessing...did he want more from you?" asked Myrtle.

"He sure did. And, at that point, I was one-hundred-percent in pursuit of Felix. I told Tobin 'thanks, but no thanks.' Sometimes he took that advice and sometimes he kept on trying to persuade me to go out with him again. I guess he was lonely, like you said."

"What did Felix think about you being one-hundred-percent in pursuit of him? Was he all right with that?"

Sybil's eyes clouded. "No, he never was. He's been happy to go see a movie with me or to eat supper with me, but I'm starting to think that's all he wants. The more I'm running at him, the more he's running away. It made me feel real desperate, too. Like when Cosette started flirting with him—that drove me crazy, because I didn't feel like I had enough of a hold on Felix for him to be able to ignore her flirting."

"How have things been going lately? Have y'all been going out?" asked Myrtle.

"We haven't done a single thing. I've been calling him and dropping by the office and dropping by his house and he's been too busy or has just ignored the phone call or my knock altogether. Although I know he's there, because I'd driven by and seen his car there minutes before." Sybil looked hurt.

Sybil seemed to be a first rate stalker, with not a single clue that that's what she was.

"The last day or two, *I've* seen my caller ID and know he's trying to reach me, out of the blue, without returning any of the calls I made to him. I'm wondering if he's wanting to break up with me," said Sybil, looking worried.

It sounded as if there wasn't anything really to break up. "You didn't answer the phone when he called?"

"I had a bad feeling about it, so I didn't. I've been avoiding him myself." Sybil sighed.

Myrtle said, "This is sort of off-topic, but do you have any idea why Felix might have been spotted walking briskly down the street with a suit on? Looking out of sorts?"

Sybil frowned. "You mean on the day of Tobin's funeral? I can make a guess. That was the morning that his car wouldn't start and he had an early meeting with a client. He had to walk to work. It made me really mad when I found out about it because he didn't even call to ask me to drive him over. You'd think that even if we were just *friends* that he would ask for that kind of a small favor. But no. It made me think that he didn't feel our relationship was special."

This somehow irritated Myrtle. She could recognize pig-headedness when she saw it and if Felix was so determined to be left alone, by golly, maybe he should be left alone. For him not to even call poor Sybil for a ride… "You know, Sybil? You deserve better than this one-way relationship. You really do." Sybil might not be the brightest bulb and she might choose truly awful book club books, but she seemed kind.

Apparently, it hadn't occurred to Sybil that she might deserve better. An expression of surprise flitted across her face, then she said slowly, "I think you're right, Miss Myrtle. Maybe I do."

There was a peremptory knock at the door and an imperious voice called, "Sybil? I know you're in there. You have a fairly recognizable car, you know."

Sybil drew in a hissing breath. "Felix!" Her face was a mixture of longing and anxiety.

"Remember," said Myrtle. "You deserve better."

Felix pushed the front door open and gave a funny, choppy bob of his head to Myrtle. "Miss Myrtle. Sorry for barging in this way—it's only that I've been trying to reach Sybil lately and haven't been able to communicate with her. I hope you're doing well and have continued thinking about those final expenses of yours."

Myrtle clenched her teeth to keep from responding. It was Sybil's turn now.

Sybil summoned up whatever gumption she had and said briskly, "I'm glad you dropped by, Felix. I've been wanting to tell you that our—whatever we've had—is over. And I'll thank you to stop calling my house, knocking on my door, and following me around town." She raised her pointed chin and stared him down.

Felix snorted. "*Me* follow *you* around? You've got it all backwards. You're the one who's been driving *me* crazy and I've come in today to tell you to cease all contact with me."

Sybil started trembling and Myrtle stood up, feeling sore, but using her cane for support. "Your little speech is completely unnecessary since Sybil has just stated that the relationship is over. It's time for you to leave."

Felix gave Sybil a scornful look and said, "Miss Myrtle, Sybil has been stalking me all over town for weeks and...."

Sybil gave a cry. "I covered up for you at Cosette's! And this is how you treat me."

Felix's face turned purple. "You don't know what you're saying. There was no covering up."

"There was! You and I didn't leave together. And I saw you turn around and head back to Cosette's. I almost followed you."

Felix gave a high-pitched laugh. "You've lost your mind."

"Maybe, but I'm finding it again. You went back to Cosette's house. Did you kill her? Did you have an argument and she said she was going to tell people you'd had an affair? That would ruin your business, wouldn't it? In a town like this?"

Felix's face turned purple.

"Trust is awfully important in the insurance business," said Myrtle thoughtfully. "And people do talk in Bradley. They know they shouldn't gossip, but they simply can't ever seem to help themselves."

Felix took several deep breaths, nostrils flaring as he did. "You and I left together."

"In separate cars. And then you went back."

After a few moments of silence, Felix said in a halting voice, "Okay. I went back. But I only went back because I'd left my wallet there."

"A likely story." Sybil snorted.

"I certainly didn't go back to kill Cosette, of that I can assure you. Now, if things are settled between us, Sybil, I'll leave you ladies." He strode stiffly to Myrtle's front door, and then turned, one hand on the handle. "Miss Myrtle, if you'd like to talk more about those final expenses...."

She brandished her cane at him and he darted out.

After Sybil left, Myrtle decided she'd go out for a while. It was a bright, sunny day. She wanted to return the walker to Carolyn Frances with a hearty thanks-but-no-thanks. She also wanted to pop by the knitting store that Sybil had mentioned to her to see what types of yarns they had in stock. The psychic had told her to take up knitting, after all. Perhaps, for once, she should listen to someone else's advice.

Myrtle decided she would steer clear of staircases of any type or description. And that perhaps stretching her arms and legs would help her loosen up and not be so sore.

She put her knitting in her pocketbook and gripped the walker with both hands. The only way to return it appeared to be to walk it there. Myrtle set off down the street. She paced herself slowly because of her unfamiliarity with the walker.

She had just turned down a side street to head to Carolyn's house when she heard a voice beside her. Myrtle turned and saw Joan in a car next to her.

"I didn't know you got a walker!" Joan looked alarmed. "Was it your tumble down the ramp that did it to you?"

"Actually, I don't even need it. I'm in the process of returning it to the person who lent it to me. Maybe she can give it to someone who really needs a walker."

Joan said, "It looks like you're kind of awkward with it. Can I give you a lift?"

The temperature was rising outside and Myrtle realized she really wasn't particularly stable. Those things were trickier to use than they seemed. "Thanks," she said. "I think I can fold this thing up and both it and I can fit in the front, since it's not a long drive. No Noah today?"

"Noah is visiting his paw-paw right now," said Joan.

Myrtle folded the walker up quickly and climbed into the front. Joan drove off. "Thanks," said Myrtle again. "It's really heating up outside." She frowned as Joan sped up. These young people were always in such a hurry.

Something else was bothering her and Myrtle couldn't really put her finger on it. Joan kept making conversation. "It's hot, but tolerable. At least there's a bit of a breeze today. I try to get Noah out to play every day I can, and this will be one of those days I can make it happen. I think I'll pull out that plastic wading pool we have and let him play with the hose for a while. That way he can stay cool."

Myrtle was making all the appropriate *mmm-hmm* noises at all the right times as her brain worked to figure out what seemed 'off' to her.

"Where are we headed?" asked Joan.

"Hmm?"

"I wondered where we were headed," said Joan in a slightly louder voice as if Myrtle might be getting hard of hearing.

"Oh. Carolyn Frances's house." Myrtle got quiet for a moment. Then she said, "Joan, why did you say that I fell on the ramp?"

Chapter Nineteen

Joan darted a swift look across at her as she drove toward Carolyn's. "Because you did. Remember? You fell down."

"No, I was pushed," said Myrtle tiredly. "I swear to goodness I'm tired of people saying I fell. But you're the first person to mention my falling down on the *ramp*. Everyone else has said *stairs*. Even the newspaper printed that I'd fallen on the stairs."

Joan gave a short laugh. "Guess I had ramps on the brain for some reason, that's all."

Myrtle said in a mulling voice, "There have been some other things lately that have made me wonder. Like the way your father swore up and down that he never had an argument with Tobin…until he was confronted by more proof than we'd already had. And the way that you swore you never came back to your mother's drop-in—until witnesses placed you there. There are a whole lot of unanswered questions, aren't there?"

"Oh, I don't *think* so." Joan's voice was becoming icy.

Myrtle added, "One other thing. Your father had said he didn't even know about the croquet mallets because he never went outside and didn't have the slightest interest in gardening. But then he was able to tell me that I needed to have Dusty spray my whiteflies on the underside of my gardenia bushes. That's kind of odd, don't you think?"

"He was only trying to be helpful," said Joan briskly. "If you want to keep your whiteflies, then ignore him. That's probably what Mother did."

"But I don't *want* to ignore him, that's the thing. I want to have Dusty take care of my bushes. I just want to know how he knew so much about it."

"Probably listening to Mother," said Joan with a shrug.

"I was under the impression that he didn't listen to her much."

"I'd say that's a fair assessment. It's how they made their relationship work, I guess." Joan's hands were tight on the wheel.

"And, Joan, you're a nurturing mother. If you'd seen your mother lying on the ground when you returned to the party, it would have been pure instinct for you to run over to see if she were all right," said Myrtle.

"She wasn't that kind of mother," muttered Joan.

"But for your curiosity, at least, Joan! You'd have run over," Myrtle was certain of this and that certainty flowed into her voice. "It simply doesn't make any sense. On my soap opera—*Tomorrow's Promise*—Kristin and her mother were squabbling over her wedding plans. They've been at odds with each other for the last ten episodes. But if it were Kristin's mom lying on the ground, she'd at least check for a *pulse*. You'd do that even with a total stranger."

"Oh sure. Use a soap opera to try to make sense out of a murder investigation." Joan snorted.

Myrtle continued, "With the timing of the events, you'd have returned when Erma, Sybil, and Felix were leaving. You'd have gone around the side of the house. If you *had* seen your mother lying on the ground then and *had* run over, as I feel strongly that you would have, then I'd have seen you hovering over the body. That's how tight that series of events is."

"But you didn't. You didn't see me hovering over her body."

"Because you killed her and left. I must have discovered her a couple of minutes after that," said Myrtle slowly. She needed to get out of this car. Joan had sped up, though, and Myrtle knew that jumping out of a rapidly moving car could engender enough broken bones to be just as fatal as whatever Joan might plan to do to her.

"But Tobin saw you, didn't he? He saw what happened, although he didn't put two-and-two together until he found out Cosette had been murdered. He was surreptitiously putting that bag of trash out on the porch. So Tobin's lying low, watching the party, and sees you go around the side of the house. Maybe he also saw you still gripping the croquet mallet—is that it? You might even have forgotten you were still holding it and had to go back around the house to return it. That would have been pretty definite evidence from an eyewitness, wouldn't it?"

Joan pressed her lips together.

"Tobin has a long-standing grudge with your family, so he decides to make y'all suffer a little. Instead of merely going to the police to report what he'd seen, he thinks that blackmailing the family would be restitution for all his troubles with Cosette." Myrtle's voice still rang with certainty. It made perfect sense.

Joan snorted. "Like I have any money for blackmailers. A single mom living through handouts from her parents. And I already told you that Dad was in a real hole, too."

"But Lucas and Cosette seemed to have money. If Tobin had wanted money, and I believe he did, then he would have talked to Lucas about it. Besides, Cosette had bragged around town that Lucas valued her so much that he'd taken out a large life insurance policy on her. Not only did Lucas *currently* seem to have more money than you, but he was about to come into a *great deal* more money. Plus, you are his only child and the mother of his only grandchild."

Joan sneered, "So, on the very morning of my mother's funeral, while I'm toting my child around with me, I drove by the graveyard, saw Tobin, and ran up to kill him with a shovel. Right!"

"Wrong. Lucas knew what you'd done, although he must have denied it hotly to Tobin. He'd already suffered the loss of his wife—a tremendous one, despite how she treated him. Your father couldn't bear to suffer the loss of his daughter to prison, as well. And what would happen to Noah? Lucas felt driven to protect you both. He knew that Tobin maintained the cemetery grounds and the funeral home may even have mentioned that the time of the service would have to be a particular hour because Tobin would be working on the grounds before then," said Myrtle.

Joan stared straight ahead.

"Your father would have gone early to the graveyard and had to wait quietly for a moment to confront Tobin. As his luck would have it, Tobin was working in a shaded, woody area to the side of the cemetery. Lucas had more cover for his crime in the shade. He acted quickly, and with the element of surprise on his side, was able to whack Tobin hard with the shovel as he knelt to work. Tobin probably never knew what hit him."

Joan stayed silent.

Myrtle continued, "I was asking too many questions, I guess. Making you uncomfortable. I even visited Felix to ask about the life insurance. You felt like you had too much to lose, and were willing to take some risks to protect your dad and yourself. I was zoning in on the areas you were hoping to keep secret. You saw your chance to do away with me by shoving me down the ramp, figuring that even if I didn't break anything, I'd probably either be injured enough to give up my investigating, or scared off totally."

Here, Joan did jump in. "Sure. So I shove an old lady, trying to do her grievous harm, when I've got my small child with me. Noah would have called out, you know."

"I'm imagining that Noah was fairly tired out after his previous trip to the library that day—when I was there picking out a book club selection. Children that age still frequently need an afternoon nap. He certainly got very sleepy when I was babysitting him. I'm guessing that Noah did take a nap—and that you slipped out of the house while he was sleeping to follow me for a while. You saw the perfect opportunity to either scare me to death or to injure me in a way that would shut down my ability to investigate." Myrtle looked sternly at Joan. "And now I'd like you to tell me where we're going."

Joan gave that strangled laugh again. "Well, I can't exactly silence you for good, right in the middle of downtown Bradley, Miss Myrtle. That would hardly go unnoticed in our gossipy little town, now would it? No, we have to take a bit of a car ride. You'll simply *conveniently disappear*."

Myrtle shivered. "You've got to rethink this, Joan. You're desperate now and you're not thinking clearly. Someone must have seen me get into your car. You won't get away with this, you know."

"Maybe they did see you and maybe they didn't. But I'll have to take that chance. You've already got it all figured out, haven't you?" Joan's voice sounded frantic.

Myrtle took a deep breath. "Think of Noah, Joan. You'll only make things worse by killing me. With the death of your mother, you could even claim it was in the heat of the moment…which it probably was. When you're caught and charged with your mother's death…*and* my death…things will be that much worse for you. You might never even get out of prison. Might not be able to hold Noah again. Let's turn around, Joan. Let's go straight to Red and tell him what happened. You'll get off so much easier, I know it."

Joan's only response was to drive faster and head farther out of town. Myrtle remembered that you were never supposed to go to a second location with someone who took you by force. In her situation, though, she couldn't exactly launch herself out of the vehicle. And when she'd gotten into the car to begin with, Joan hadn't been the frightening stranger that she'd become over the course of this car ride.

After driving a few more miles, Joan pulled to a stop in a secluded area. All Myrtle could see were kudzu vines everywhere, and dilapidated, deserted farm buildings overgrown with bushes and weeds. "Get out of the car," Joan said icily. Myrtle hesitated and Joan pulled a knife from her pocketbook. "Get out of the car," she repeated.

Myrtle slowly opened the passenger door and got out, pulling her walker out with her.

Joan said, "Drop that walker. You're not going to need it now." She walked around the car and brandished the knife at Myrtle. "Drop it and keep walking. Head to those woods over there."

"If you want me to *make it* to the woods, you'll let me use that walker," said Myrtle with a hint of asperity in her voice.

"You just said that you didn't need the walker and you were set to return it," said Joan, narrowing her eyes at Myrtle suspiciously.

"That was then, this is now. You're wanting me to go off-road. I'm absolutely fine when I'm in my house or walking down the pavement. But going off through a field and then through the woods?" Myrtle shook her head vehemently.

"All right," snapped Joan. "Only because I don't want to have to drag your body all the way to the woods."

For once, Myrtle was grateful for her big-boned, tall frame. She unfolded the walker and started heading for the woods, feeling very much as Marie Antoinette must have felt on her way to the guillotine. Her only hope was to stall for a bit. Could she somehow stall enough until she could get that knife away from Joan?

"Had you planned on killing your mother all along, Joan? It seems more of a spur-of-the-moment thing," said Myrtle casually as she walked toward the woods.

"No, *clearly* it wasn't planned, since I'd never have chosen a time when Mother was hosting a huge soiree full of potential witnesses." Now Joan was sneering again.

Myrtle was desperate to buy a bit of time. "Why did you come back, then? Why go around the side of the house? Why was your mother outside at all?"

Joan heaved a sigh. "I came back to get Noah. I ran my errand and then realized I was exhausted. As usual. Mother had that effect on me. She was tying me down to a life I didn't want, just like she'd done every day of my life. Mother always wanted me to be the pretty one, the one with all the dates, the one with all the answers. Someone who was smart, the perfect hostess, *and* beautiful. I was none of those things. Well…I might have been smart."

"You weren't even interested in those things, were you?" asked Myrtle.

Joan's laugh sounded bitter. "Maybe I would have been if I'd had the looks to carry them off. But I was always socially awkward, and Mother kept signing me up for things like etiquette classes and ballroom dancing. It was pure torment for me since I was a total wallflower."

"She had big plans for you, didn't she?" asked Myrtle.

Joan's voice was gritty. "She was planning on my being nothing less than the first lady. Note that she never planned on my being *president*. I was only supposed to be the perfect accompaniment. But I was not fitting her mold. Then I married a plumber and she really flipped out."

"Did she finally give up on your becoming something you weren't, then?"

"She sure did. Even when I became divorced. I think she finally realized I was never going to be a society matron," said Joan.

Myrtle asked, "Then she started transferring all those hopes and dreams onto Noah when he was born?"

"Immediately. Of course, her plans for him were that he'd end up a CEO of a major corporation. I could see what she was thinking, just by looking at her. The night of the party, I went around the side of the house to try to enter through the back since the front door was clogged with people. Mother was in the kitchen at the time, I guess, and saw me coming. She came outside and started fussing at me because she'd popped into that bedroom and heard Noah telling the sitter about some dumb TV show he'd seen at home." Joan's voice hardened at the memory.

"Your mother was complaining about your parenting?" asked Myrtle.

"Oh, that was constant. Constant! This time, though, it really got to me. Why *shouldn't* he be able to relax and watch some of the same shows his preschool friends are watching? Why couldn't he have any downtime? I'd had enough. The mallet set was right next to us and without even thinking, I reached down, grabbed a mallet, and struck her with it."

Myrtle shivered at the look of satisfaction in Joan's eyes. Then she took a deep breath. She needed to act while Joan was absorbed in her thoughts. Myrtle swiftly reached out and grabbed the knife, pulling it toward her as hard as she could.

Joan's reflexes were the reflexes of the young. Her grip automatically tightened on the knife. A sneer pulled at the corners of her mouth. "Good try, Miss Myrtle. You get points for trying." She yanked her arm and pulled the knife back, hoisting it high in the air, ready to strike.

"Hold it right there," said a grim but shaking voice.

Joan whipped her head around toward the voice and Myrtle's eyes widened.

It was Tina. Kim. Whoever. The cub reporter. She was holding that toy gun out in two trembling hands and it no longer looked like a toy. It looked dangerous.

Joan croaked, "Who are you?"

Myrtle said, "She's a member of the Bradley, North Carolina Press Corps. I think your dirty little secret is out for good, Joan."

Joan lunged at Kim. Myrtle quickly shoved the walker at Joan's legs, bringing her down to the ground. Joan gave a furious shriek as she tried to untangle herself from the walker. Myrtle nodded to the gun and hastily asked Kim, "Do you know how to use that thing?"

Kim, white-faced, nodded uncertainly at Myrtle.

"*Would* you use that thing?" asked Myrtle urgently.

Kim stared wordlessly at Myrtle. Myrtle held out her hand and Kim quickly gave her the gun…but dropped it before she could hand it over.

Myrtle quickly stooped, using the prostrate walker to help her bend down. Joan was simultaneously grappling around in the muddy earth for the gun. Kim was frozen in place.

Myrtle's fingers knocked it closer to Joan, who was able to get her fingers nearly to the point where she could grasp the pistol. Myrtle swiftly reached inside her purse and brought out a knitting needle, stabbing Joan in the arm. Joan pulled back with a howl of pain and Myrtle crawled to grab the gun. She sat, panting on the ground, aiming the weapon at Joan who was seething near her.

"Joan, listen up. I *will* use this gun. I don't want to, though. My daddy taught me how to shoot many, many years ago and he told me to always shoot to kill. Don't make me do it," said Myrtle, pointing the miniature gun at Joan, who slumped, looking defeated.

Kim was looking slightly sick. Myrtle said quickly, "Kim, could you call Red? Tell him what's going on, just in case Joan tries anything." Kim shot Joan an alarmed look and Myrtle added, "Although I don't think she will."

Chapter Twenty

"What I don't understand," said Red. "Is why that reporter just happened to be out there in the middle of nowhere with you."

They were back at Myrtle's house—Kim too. She'd needed a ride to get back out of there since she was still too shaken up to get behind a wheel. Red had taken only a few minutes to arrive—he must have been flying. Now Myrtle was settled in her living room with a glass of sherry and Kim had gone to the restroom, which was why Red was questioning Myrtle now about it.

"I might have given her a lead," said Myrtle.

"A lead that took her out to the middle of nowhere? No wonder the girl carries a gun," said Red.

"I was only trying to keep her from being so underfoot all the time. She was driving me nuts, covering this story and then doing those ridiculous follow-ups on my 'fall.'" Myrtle sighed.

Red looked away at the mention of the fall. "Yes, well. Okay, well, sorry about my not believing that you were pushed, Mama. Joan already admitted she'd done that to the state police, apparently."

"I guess it did sound like I was making it up instead of owning up to unsteadiness," said Myrtle grudgingly.

"So she was driving you nuts and you told her…?" Red looked questioningly at her.

Myrtle cleared her throat. "I recommended that she go talk to Darla Covington. It was a fool's errand."

"I'll say! I bet Darla sent Kim off with a flea in her ear. She lives out in the boonies for a reason—and it's not because she likes company. That wasn't a very nice thing to do, Mama."

"Well, right now it looks like a stroke of genius," said Myrtle. "After all, Kim apparently got lost after Darla turned her away. She saw Joan's car and decided to ask for directions. Although I thought all the young people had GPS on their phones or something." Myrtle frowned.

"They do. But Kim's phone was out of range. That's what she said when I talked to her a few minutes ago. I knew what happened *after* she talked to Darla; I just didn't know how she came to be out there. Thank goodness she *was* out there, Mama, or you'd be deader than a doornail by now."

Myrtle shivered and took a sustaining sip of sherry as Kim came back out. Red looked at her and said, "Kim, I appreciate your talking to me. I think I've gotten all the information from you that I need. I have asked a sergeant from the state police to give you a lift back to your car if you're feeling more relaxed. He should be outside in a cruiser. I'll let you know if I need to talk with you again."

Kim nodded. "I'll give you my cell number. I don't think I'll be sticking around. If I couldn't handle what happened today, I shouldn't even be in this business. Now I've found out that I didn't even get the details of your mother's fall right. You said that Joan pushed her and that she was on a ramp, not the stairs?" She shook her head in self-disgust. "Miss Myrtle, do you think you could write up this story for me? I don't even want to relive what happened today."

Myrtle felt a twinge of guilt. She was the one who'd practically set the whole thing up. She nodded and said, "Kim…you do have some talent, you know." The words were hard to say. "I mean—you did get the details of my fall wrong, so you do need to make sure you double-check your information before you publish it. But you write well."

Kim made a face and shook her head again.

"Okay, maybe crime reporting isn't your thing. There are other types of things you could write. Do you have any interest at all in lifestyle reporting? Fashion, fitness, the arts, things like that?" asked Myrtle.

Kim nodded. "I sure do. But I wasn't sure I could get those types of jobs without some experience first. That's why I'm here."

Red raised a questioning eyebrow at his mother.

"I have a cousin, Josephine Stringfellow," said Myrtle thoughtfully. "She's the lifestyle editor at the newspaper in Macon, Georgia. Not only is she my cousin, but I also taught her English when she was young. Plus, I used my contacts to help her find her first job many years ago. I do believe she owes me a favor."

Kim was starting to grin now. "Really? You'd do that for me?"

"I owe you one," said Myrtle. "Really."

After Kim left, Red sighed and rubbed his eyes tiredly. "I really don't know how you keep ending up in the middle of these cases, Mama. But I sure am glad this one is over with."

"Do you have any updates on Lucas?" asked Myrtle. "And what on earth have y'all done with poor Noah? What's going to happen to him? I understood that Joan's ex-husband wants nothing to do with the little guy."

Red said, "We sent a cop out to arrest Lucas. The little guy was there, but there was a female officer from the state police that sat with him in the kitchen and gave him a snack so he didn't see his grandfather being taken away. My understanding is that the aunt—Hazel?—was going to take Noah, at least temporarily."

"Oh good," said Myrtle, feeling more relieved than she thought she would. "He is a nice boy. And Hazel seemed very competent. That sounds as though it will work out well for Noah. How was Lucas?"

"Shaken." Red shook his head. "The cops I talked to said he broke down and cried like a baby. He was still grieving for Cosette and also grieving Joan's arrest, even though she was the one who made him lose his wife. Even so, she and Noah were really all he'd had left."

"Sad," said Myrtle. Then she straightened up in her chair. "Wait. No, we shouldn't feel sorry for him, really. He shouldn't have killed Tobin. Poor Tobin."

"But 'poor Tobin' was blackmailing him," reminded Red. "In a way, Lucas was a victim, too. And Tobin wasn't the great guy everybody thought he was."

Red's handheld radio that was belted to his waist started making noises. He took it off and listened for a moment. "I need to get back to the office," he said. "Are you okay? Are you *sure* you're okay?"

"I am," said Myrtle. "I'm surprised I am, but I am. Thank you," she added graciously.

"I suppose I'll take that walker back to Carolyn," said Red. "Since you weren't actually unsteady when you took that tumble."

"It might be muddy," said Myrtle. "But tell her it helped save my life…in a most unexpected way."

"All right. Let me know if you need anything. Actually, let me text Elaine real quick and get her to come over and visit for a while to settle your nerves some more."

"I should thank Elaine for bringing me those knitting needles," muttered Myrtle. The psychic had been right about her needing to take up knitting. The thought sent a shiver up Myrtle's spine.

There was a tap on the door and Red walked over to answer it. "It's Miles," he called over his shoulder. "Are you receiving company?"

"Miles isn't company. He's just…Miles. Go ahead and let him in. And don't bother Elaine—if Miles is going to be here, I don't want to take her away from stuff she needs to do at home."

Red said, "Okay. Although I know she's going to be dying to check in with you. Maybe she'll drop by later." He opened the door and greeted Miles and then walked away.

Miles watched him out the front window. "Looks like he's taking that walker of yours away. You've got to feel good about that."

"You know, Miles, I feel almost fond of that walker now."

Miles raised his eyebrows and Myrtle filled him in on the whole story. She'd needed a wee refill of sherry to get through the toughest parts—as reinforcement.

Miles and Myrtle sat quietly for a moment. "That's quite a story," said Miles finally.

"It sure is," said Myrtle fervently.

"And you came out of the experience alive and well. And even smoothly handled the dicey situation with the cub reporter." Miles gave her an admiring look. "I must say, that was a stroke of genius on your part, sending her away by giving her what she wanted. That was a very mature way to handle it."

"Well, at my age, I *should* be mature, for heaven's sake," said Myrtle. "Besides, I'd originally felt that the girl was too cocky and needed to be knocked down a peg. And she *was* knocked down a peg, although I had nothing to do with it. Everything worked out really well."

"What will you do now?"

"I'm going to write this story up. It's going to be the best article the *Bradley Bugle* has ever seen," said Myrtle, standing up and heading to her computer. "I started the story the other day, but now it's going to have a spellbinding ending."

“Guess I should head along home then,” said Miles. But when Myrtle turned to look at him, he seemed to be in no hurry to move from the overstuffed armchair he was in.

“Why not just visit for a while?” She motioned to the kitchen. “You could pour us some iced teas and when I’m done with the story, we’ll watch my tape of *Tomorrow’s Promise*. And if I get stuck on any bits of words for my article, I’ll ask you for help. You can ride shotgun.”

“Considering the circumstances, I think we should come up with a better description for my assistance. But I’m happy to stay for a while and offer a helpful synonym or two, Miles said with a smile on his face.”

And that’s how the afternoon was spent.

About the Author:

Elizabeth's latest book, *Knot What it Seams* , released February 2013 and *Rubbed Out* launched July 2, 2013, under her Riley Adams pen name. Elizabeth writes the Memphis Barbeque series for Penguin/Berkley (as Riley Adams), the Southern Quilting mysteries for Penguin/NAL, and the Myrtle Clover series for Midnight Ink and independently.

She blogs at Mystery Writing is Murder which was named by *Writer's Digest* as one of the 101 Best Websites for Writers for 2010—2013.

Other Works by the Author:

Myrtle Clover Series in Order:

Pretty is as Pretty Dies
Progressive Dinner Deadly
A Dyeing Shame
A Body in the Backyard
Death at a Drop-In
Coming soon: A Body at Book Club

Southern Quilting Mysteries in Order:

Quilt or Innocence
Knot What it Seams
Quilt Trip (December 2013)

Memphis Barbeque Mysteries in Order (*Written as Riley Adams*):

Delicious and Suspicious
Finger Lickin' Dead
Hickory Smoked Homicide
Rubbed Out

Where to Connect With Elizabeth:

Facebook: Elizabeth Spann Craig Author
Riley Adams, Author
Twitter: @elizabethscraig
Website: www.elizabethspanncraig.com
Blog: www.mysterywritingismurder.blogspot.com

Chapter One of *A Body at Book Club*

Myrtle was drowsily watching her favorite soap opera when her viewing was suddenly interrupted by a cat's screaming wail and the sound of dogs snapping and growling.

"Pasha!" she gasped, struggling to her feet from the padded softness of her armchair and knocking a half-finished crossword puzzle from her lap. Grabbing her cane in one hand and a water pitcher she'd poured after a salty lunch, she hurried out the front door.

Two large dogs were on her front walk, snapping at and nosing a black, frightened cat that was trapped between them and fighting to get out. Myrtle bellowed, "Stop!" and threw cold water at the animals. They stopped, swinging their heads around to stare at Myrtle. The cat bolted away as fast as she could go.

"Bad dogs!" snapped Myrtle sternly, brandishing her cane at them and they instantly put their tails between their legs and lowered their ears.

Myrtle's police chief son lived directly across the street from her and she saw his door fly open at all the commotion. "You okay, Mama?" he called.

"I wasn't the one in the dog fight—it was Pasha. Now she's run off and I don't know if she's hurt or not." Myrtle was exasperated to hear a note of panic in her voice. It was surprising how important that feral cat had become to her.

Red dodged back inside, finally hurrying out again with his shoes on and his keys in his hand. He also held something that Myrtle couldn't really see. He walked purposefully across the street. "There *is* a leash law in this town. I sure wish folks would remember that." His once-red hair, now mostly gray, stuck straight up on the side of his head and he blinked as if he'd just awakened from a nap.

"You know how the old-timers are here in Bradley," said Myrtle. "They just ignore whichever laws inconvenience them. I don't know who owns these dogs and they don't have tags on them." She started calling for Pasha. "Kitty, kitty, kitty?" Her heart was still pounding and she breathed deeply to settle herself down.

"Pasha's too smart to come out before she thinks she's safe, Mama. Maybe after I've put these dogs in the police cruiser, she'll come." Red whistled to the dogs and clapped his hands, and then he held out whatever he'd been carrying and the animals obediently followed him as if he were the pied piper.

"Treats? For bad dogs?" Myrtle was outraged.

"Well, they're just acting like dogs, Mama. And I've got to get them into my car—I figured hot dogs would be sure to lure them in there."

Sure enough, the dogs were all over those bits of hot dogs. Once they were in the car, Red slammed the back doors and walked around to the driver's side.

"You're arresting those dogs?" asked Myrtle.

"Just taking them down to the station to hang out there until someone claims them. That way I can also remind the owners about the leash law," said Red.

Myrtle watched as he herded the dogs into the back of the police car. He backed out of his driveway and then rolled down his window. "Mama, I'll help you look for the cat when I come back, okay?"

Myrtle raised her eyebrows in surprise. "I thought you weren't exactly Pasha's number-one fan."

"I'm not. Shoot, Mama, it's a feral cat. How am I supposed to feel about my octogenarian mother hanging out with a wild animal? But it's better for me to be stooping under bushes to look for her, instead of you. You're unsteady on your feet as it is."

Myrtle glared at him. He was interfering, as usual. "I'm just fine on my feet, Red. This cane just helps me move faster, that's all. Go on to the station. I'll get Miles to help me."

He drove off and Myrtle stuck her tongue out at his car as it left. She decided to leave her friend Miles alone for the time being. His guilty pleasure was watching her soap opera—she'd gotten him hooked on it, and it would just be wrapping up now. Myrtle looked around her. "Kitty, kitty, kitty?" she called, bending down to look under bushes and neighbors' cars.

Which direction had Pasha run off in? Myrtle had to admit she wasn't sure, she'd just seen her run. Maybe she'd run far away, making sure she was well out of the way of those dogs. Myrtle walked back inside, opened a can of albacore tuna, and kept looking. After scanning her yard and her neighbors' yards, she moved down to the next block of houses, calling as she walked and hoping that the smell of the tuna might tempt the poor cat out of hiding.

The sun blazed down on her and the early-summer humidity felt oppressive. Myrtle thought she saw some movement in the bushes of a shady yard and walked right into the yard, calling and holding out the can. A squirrel scampered away and Myrtle gave an exasperated sigh.

She jumped a little as an authoritative voice barked, "Hey there. Miss Myrtle. What are you doing?"

Myrtle looked up to see Rose Mayfield standing in her front door, hands on her hips, and an impatient look on her face. "I'm looking for my lost cat, that's all," said Myrtle.

"For heaven's sake. How will it help the cat if you have a heat stroke in my front yard?" Rose looked imperiously down her aristocratic nose at Myrtle. With her thin frame, brunette hair laced with gray, and angular features, Rose had always reminded her of a particularly cranky Katharine

Hepburn. "Come on inside," she said briskly, holding the door open. "Have some water, cool down, then you can find your pet."

"She's not a pet," said Myrtle as she walked in, sitting down on an antique sofa and carefully setting down her can of tuna. "She's a feral cat that I've befriended. Pasha's very sweet, though."

"I'm sure she is," said Rose, cutting her off as she quickly walked into the kitchen, wet down a dishcloth with cool water, and handed it over to Myrtle. The look on her face indicated that *she* wouldn't allow *her* elderly mother to *have* a feral cat. "I'll get you some ice water. Please have a seat."

Myrtle didn't like being lectured, but this time she bit her tongue and didn't argue with the authoritative Rose. That's because she discovered that she *was*, actually, thirsty. She gulped down the water Rose brought her and then gave a begrudging apology for imposing, since Rose, arms crossed in front of her, looked so incredibly put-out.

"Oh, it's fine," said Rose impatiently. "Your visit will distract me from the murder going on next door."

"Murder?" asked Myrtle with quickening interest.

Read the rest of *A Body at Book Club* when it releases in Fall 2013